THE

GOOD

DIVIDE

A NOVEL

MG Press
http://midwestgothic.com/mgpress

ISBN: 978-1-944850-00-5

Cover design © Lauren Crawford

Cover photo © Dorothea Lange

Library of Congress, Prints & Photographs Division, FSA/OWI Collection, LC-DIG-fsa-8b31749

A mother in California who with her husband and her two children will be returned to Oklahoma by the Relief Administration. This family had lost a two-year-old baby during the winter as a result of exposure.

March, 1937, the Farm Security Administration/Office of War Information Black & White.

Back cover photo © Jamey Davidsmeyer

Author photo © Bethany Kohoutek

THE
GOOD
DIVIDE

A NOVEL

KALI VANBAALE

For my parents, Myron and Sue.

For giving me such a nice beginning to my own story.

And oftentimes such cursing returns again upon the head of him that curses, like a bird that returns again to its own nest.

Geoffrey Chaucer, "The Parson's Tale" from *The Canterbury Tales*

MISTRESSES

A farm is like a mistress, a passively tolerated extramarital distraction that keeps husbands out well past dark and wives pacing kitchen floors with cranky babies on their hips and supper plates gone cold at the table. We farm wives learn early on to put up with the other woman and her demanding, petulant needs, while our own play second fiddle or go unattended altogether. It is just the nature of farm life.

One hundred and ten acres of rich, black Wisconsin dirt has consumed attention from some member of our family for more than a century. Like the line of inhabitants before me—before us, I should say—we have experienced what seems to be an invisible curse on the land, first settled by an immigrant couple from Germany who lost babies three winters in a row in their drafty cabin home. Another family battled an outbreak of tuberculosis and then, according to my late father-in-law's conspiracy theory, a massive grass fire set by a jealous neighbor around the time of the Civil War. There was a six-year-old girl who drowned in the pond while trying to catch tadpoles, and a father with nine children who hung himself from a tree after a tornado wiped out his entire cattle herd and hay barn, as the story goes in an old newspaper clipping.

Finally, there were the two cousins who married sisters in a double ceremony, twin sisters with rumored telepathic communication. It was the cousins who built the identical white houses that mirror each other just across the drive, anchored in perfect symmetry with equal amounts of yard and within shouting distance so the sisters could raise their families together. But only one of the women would ever produce children, and just one boy out of five offspring. He would inherit the entire farm, two houses and surrounding land, adding concrete silos that reached forty feet into the sky like bony fingers stabbing at the clouds, and later, electricity in the barn and the first gas-powered tractor to work the fields. He would pass all this down to his two boys, upon his death from lung cancer, before cigarettes came with warnings on the carton. The brothers would share this inheritance with their wives, she and I, two strangers brought together by the mistress in our respective marriages to live within feet of each other, separated only by a single gravel divide.

Each morning I lie in my bed under the comforting heaviness of blankets and quilts, and wait for the slap of her hand on the other side of the wall, her signal to let me know that she is awake and needs to use the toilet. It is a morning just like the last and hundreds before that. We are both old and still alive and face yet another day together. So it has gone for many years. You reap what you sow, my mother used to say.

Our beds rest on different sides of the same wall, so when she beats her good hand against our shared slab of chipped plaster, the steady *slap slap* is next to my head, every morning, five-thirty, an alarm clock I can't turn off.

She can no longer write and shows no interest in the television or books. She mostly sits in front of the picture window and stares at the farm, at the white barns and houses outlined against the horizon. Sometimes I talk to her, feeling lonely and desperate to hear the sound of another human voice, even if it is my own. I tell her stories about the farm that I can still remember after all these years. Maybe she listens, maybe not. I prattle on, regardless.

We share not only that chipped wall, but also the same useless wish to lay the blame for our misfortunes onto the mistress in our lives, the farm. It's easier that way, always easier, to blame the mistress. A tree falls the way it leans, my mother used to say.

Sometimes, I catch her staring at me while I do whatever it is I am doing, waiting for me to wait on her—clip a nail, wipe her nose, fetch her a sweater—and sometimes I wonder if she is thinking about that night.

So I clip the nail, wipe her nose, fetch the sweater.

I don't complain. Lord knows I owe her that much.

CHAPTER 1

July 4, 1963

Jean Krenshaw watched as her brother-in-law's Chevy Delray finally rolled into the driveway amid a swirling cloud of gritty summer dust that settled upon the rustling corn stalks in the surrounding fields. He was late.

Jean stood behind a row of folding tables overloaded with grilled meat and bowls of fruit salads, small legions of flies crawling and buzzing along the lips of the containers. She glanced down the long line of friends and neighbors waiting under the shade of a hundred-year-old oak tree to fill a plate. This year's Fourth of July picnic would be the biggest yet. Farmers from all over the area had come to see the Krenshaw Dairy's modern milking machine, the first in the county.

Jean waved a spatula covered in whipped cream to get her husband's attention as he dumped a cup of water over an angry flame leaping off the grill.

"Jim!" she called.

Jim looked up and squinted at his wife through a rolling cloud of smoke.

"More hotdogs," she mouthed and lifted an empty plate, catching a scent of charred meat from across the yard. Jim nodded and brandished the barbeque poker at her with a playful grin. Jean's gaze lifted once more in search of the black car, now obscured by the numerous vehicles congesting the driveway and yard.

Reverend Iverson shuffled his way through the line,

dropping several scoops of cole slaw onto his plate.

"I'm looking forward to seeing the new milker," he said. A small breeze lifted one edge of the dark hairpiece atop his head and he flattened it back down with a lightning quick reflex, nearly dumping the food from his plate.

"Oh, yes." Jean nodded and bit into a crunchy dill pickle while averting her eyes. "He and Jim are planning to do a demonstration."

She would have to tell Tommy about the reverend's latest hair mishap, something she knew he would get a kick out of since he regularly cracked toupee jokes during church services. *Of course he doesn't look his age. Toupees don't go gray...*

Jean craned her neck to look over the reverend's head, distracted by the Chevy now parked under a tree at the edge of the yard. The driver's door swung open and Tommy's tall frame emerged, outfitted in the usual denim jeans, white T-shirt, and faded blue Cubs baseball cap. He waved and flashed a particular smile at Jean—the sheepish version that usually bought him forgiveness for being late.

As she was about to wave him over, Tommy rushed to the passenger side of the car and held the door open. One tanned bare leg materialized, followed by another connected to the petite frame of a woman with long, glossy black hair. He tenderly guided the young woman by the elbow and laughed at something she was saying.

Jean shook her head. Another girl.

Tommy and the woman hooked index fingers, like two fishing lures tangled in a tackle box, as he led her into the crowd. Jean watched the smiles and handshakes of neighbors, the nods of welcome and more smiles. Patchy old farmers in overalls and seed corn hats jumped up from their sagging lawn chairs to greet the barefoot girl wearing a gauzy broom skirt and layers of beaded necklaces.

"Jean." Jim nudged his wife in the side with a platter of shriveled, blackened wieners. "They're a little overdone."

"Who's that?" Jean asked, gesturing to Tommy's guest, though she usually didn't pay too much attention to Tommy's girls since they didn't stay around very long.

Jim shielded his eyes with one hand. "Oh, that's Liz."

Before Jean could respond, Jim's mother, Bonnie, dropped an empty glass pitcher onto the table.

"We're out of iced tea," she said wearily. With a tissue from her brassiere strap, she mopped rivulets of sweat from the deep crevices of wrinkled skin encasing her thick neck.

Jean put the pitcher upright and turned back to Jim. "You've met her?"

"Who are you talking about?" Bonnie asked.

"Liz." Jim lifted his arm to point but Jean slapped his hand down.

"Oh, right, Tommy's girlfriend," Bonnie said.

Jean's face blanched. "Girlfriend? You..."

"We had lunch in town a few weeks ago. Nice enough. She's dark, though. Ethnic of some sort."

"Ma, you can't say that anymore," Jim said.

"What?" Bonnie shrugged. She expectantly held the pitcher out to Jean. "Iced tea? Reverend Iverson is waiting for a glass."

"Of course," Jean said, and hurried to the house.

Inside, she filled the pitcher at her kitchen sink and dunked a bundle of tea bags, watching the party from the open window. She thought about what Bonnie had just said. *Girlfriend.* Tommy never called them his girlfriends. He was always careful to say, "This is my friend, Mary." Or "I'd like you to meet my date, Kathy." And he certainly never introduced them to his mother.

Jean lifted the café curtain with the tip of her finger and watched Tommy and the girl stroll around the yard, their heads tilted toward each other as they talked. The word sank in further. Girlfriend. There had only been one girl in ten years Tommy had pointedly called his girlfriend.

An image of that long, blonde hair fanned out across the back seat of the cab flashed through her mind. Jean shuddered and forced her attention back to the tea. She couldn't think about that today.

When Jean returned to the food table, Bonnie had clearly grown impatient.

"Finally," she said. She took the pitcher, thrust a slotted spoon dripping with cantaloupe juice into Jean's hand, and marched back into the shade of the oak tree to join Reverend Iverson.

Jim delivered another plate of meat to the table. "He's coming over to introduce you to her," he whispered into Jean's ear as Tommy and the girl approached the table.

"You could've said something to me," Jean said, fidgeting with the collar of her blouse. She pushed her heavy glasses up the bridge of her sweaty nose with her middle finger and unintentionally flipped the bird, a nervous habit she could never break.

"We're running out of buns," she snapped.

Jim stopped chewing a bite of hamburger and stared at her. "Well, don't get cross with me about it."

"I knew we would need more buns and you didn't listen to me. And you should've put out more bales of straw. There's not enough places to sit. You never listen to me!" Her voice had risen more than she intended and she suddenly felt irritated by everything.

Jim looked away, a weary expression settling into the deep lines around his eyes and mouth. He started to take another bite of his burger but stopped and threw it into the trash.

She wasn't really angry about the buns or the bales of hay. Like so many times before, she was never really angry with Jim for leaving the milk out on the counter, or forgetting his damp bath towels on the floor, or for getting up from the table before she was finished eating. But as usual, she couldn't articulate what was truly bothering her, so the tantrums persisted and she hated it when she got this way.

"Hey, Queen Jean!" Tommy waved. "I've been looking for you everywhere." He drew the girl closer to his side. "Liz, I'd like you to meet my sister-in-law, Jean."

"Nice to finally meet you." Liz reached out for Jean's hand. "Tommy talks about you all the time."

Jean accepted Liz's tiny, soft hand and, standing face-to-face, was forced to look down at the impossibly petite girl.

"Welcome to our party," Jean said, and offered a closed-mouth smile, always conscious of a yellowed front tooth from some childhood antibiotic.

"Oh, yes, what fun!" Liz moved into Jean's long shadow to block the sun, as if Jean were a tree. A breeze picked up her lustrous, thick hair, swirling it around her shoulders and face. A loose strand stuck to her lip.

Jean instinctively flattened down her own short, wind-blown hair. Up close, she guessed the girl to be in her early twenties.

"Good to see you again, Jim," Liz said, extending her hand.

"Yes, we should," Jim said and pumped the girl's thin arm, rattling the line of metal bracelets up her slight wrist.

"Um, what?" she said, with a confused but warm laugh.

A blotchy flush crept up Jim's neck and he tapped the side of his head. "Sorry, my bad ears." He had long suffered from tinnitus after years of operating loud tractors, and the ringing in his ears was always worse in noisy crowds, making him socially clumsy and self-conscious. Jean's feelings of guilt for snapping at him returned.

The tablecloth flapped in the intermittent breeze and an oak leaf dropped from the towering tree above them, landing in Jean's bowl of potato salad. She quickly plucked it out before anyone noticed.

"Would you care for some of my salad, Liz?" Jean asked,

already heaping several spoonfuls onto a plate.

"Um, sure," Liz said.

"Me too," Tommy said. "I'm starving."

Jean grinned. He had always loved her potato salad. She added more food to his plate—coleslaw, corn on the cob, watermelon cubes, several deviled eggs, all his favorites, and fixed him a burger with ketchup and onion only.

"Liz," Jim said, "I can't remember where you said you're from."

Liz nibbled on the edge of a piece of watermelon. "I live in Madison. I'm a student at the university."

Jim bobbed his head up and down but Jean knew he hadn't heard a single word of Liz's answer. He removed his mesh seed corn cap and mopped a handkerchief over the damp hair matted to his forehead. Jean caught his eye and gestured for him to wipe a bit of food out of the dark bristle of his overgrown mustache, another effort to make up for her earlier behavior.

"Liz, I didn't catch your last name," Jean said.

"Belardi."

Bingo. Italian.

"So do you live with your family in Madison, then?" Jean asked.

Liz shook her head. "No, I live by myself. I was born in a little village in Matera, Italy, but my parents passed away when I was a child. I was sent here to live with distant relatives."

"Lizzy, here, is putting herself through art school," Tommy said. "She does pottery and paintings and stuff." He beamed and pulled her against his hip.

"I'm working on my undergraduate degree in Art History," Liz said. "Though not getting much work done since I met this big distraction." She poked Tommy in the stomach with her finger. He lit a cigarette from the pack in his front t-shirt pocket and handed it to her. They passed it back and forth between each drag.

"You should hear her," Tommy said. "She talks Italian!"

Liz gently tapped the ash from the end of the cigarette. "It's all my aunt and uncle spoke at home."

"I think it's sexy as hell," Tommy said. "Even when she yells it at me."

Jean studied the couple and was struck by something unfamiliar in Tommy. He was *proud* of this girl.

"Where did you two meet?" she asked.

"Well, I'll tell ya," Tommy said. "I was up there in Madison for that dairy convention last May, when I stopped at this diner for lunch. I was sitting at the counter eating my tenderloin sandwich when this fine-looking gal sat down next to me and told me to try their apple pie 'cause they got the best apple pie in town."

"And he said that he didn't like apple pie," Liz interjected. "And I said, 'How can you not like apple pie and be American? I'm Italian and love apple pie.'"

"And then I said that I was more of a cannoli kind of man and she said that's an Italian dessert and weren't we a perfect match." They broke into joint laughter.

"Oh, isn't that something." Jean nodded her head and felt her eyes bulge with forced enthusiasm. "Isn't that something, Jim?"

"Sure, sure," Jim said.

She cocked her head at Tommy. "I didn't know you liked cannoli."

"Oh, they're grand. I get 'em from this little deal in downtown Madison every chance I get."

"Except now I can make them for him," Liz said.

"Absolutely!" Tommy planted a kiss on the side of her neck and Jean looked away, momentarily uncomfortable.

"Tom," Jim said, checking his wristwatch. "It's almost four o'clock."

"Sure thing." Tommy polished off the last bite of his

burger and handed Liz his plate. "Sorry to run off on you, Baby, but—"

"Go," Liz laughed. "I'll be fine."

"Jean, here, will bring you into the barn to watch," Tommy said. He grabbed a brownie square before he fell in step behind Jim.

Liz hesitantly glanced down at her bare feet and wriggled her toes. "To the barn, I guess."

Jean knitted her brow for a second, then cleared it and smiled. "How about we find you a pair of boots. We've got an extra pair in the barn."

Liz blushed and exhaled a long breath of relief. "Thanks. I've never been on a dairy farm before. As you can probably tell."

The women entered the stanchion barn through the milk house, an anteroom off the main building that housed the new one thousand gallon bulk tank.

"Wow," Liz said, sliding her hand along the smooth stainless steel belly of the tank. "This thing is huge!"

"We just put it in a few weeks ago," Jean said. "With the new milker we fill it once a day and a milk truck comes to empty it every night."

Jean slipped into her own pair of gumboots and found an extra pair in a cabinet for Liz. Liz stepped into them and they comically swallowed her small feet and legs up to her knees.

"They're men's," Jean said. "Sorry."

"No, no." Liz shook her head. "They're fine. Really."

Jean opened a second door from the milk house that led into the main barn and instantly met an overpowering wall of stink. Jean was used to the acrid mixture of ammonia and manure, but Liz gagged and pressed the back of her hand to her nose with an apology.

They followed the concrete center alley to where a group of neighborhood farmers had gathered around a few stalls at the far end. The stanchion barn was a massive arched-ceiling building where a herd of sixty Holsteins were housed and milked, each tied to a stall—thirty on one side, thirty on the other. Two months prior, the brothers had installed the state-of-the-art Surge Bucket Milker system and pipeline to the new tank everyone was talking about. At the center of the group, Tommy was seated on the milking stool, explaining how the automated suction cups attached to each teat of the udder. Larry, Jean's eldest son, stood alongside his father at the back of the stall holding an iodine teat dip cup.

"See, each suction tube is pressurized," Tommy was saying, "and when the milk flow slows down, they drop off automatically so the cows don't get over-milked. Cuts our milking time to five or so minutes per cow." His speech was fast and enthusiastic, like a child with a new toy.

"When she's all finished up, we just slide the Bucket over to the next cow," Jim added. "It's so smooth, even Larry here can do it." He pulled his son up to the machine to demonstrate. Larry dipped the finished cow's teats in the iodine solution and slid the Bucket Milker down the rail to the next stall. His little muscles strained with some effort, but he managed. Tommy moved the stool to the next waiting cow, her udders already dripping milk, where Larry hooked her up and started the machine. It pumped and whished to life.

"See," Jim said. "Five minutes." The audience nodded and several men clapped.

Jean crossed her arms over her chest and gave Larry a thumbs-up when he sought her out in the crowd for her approval. The new system certainly was a marvel, she thought, no matter how many times she saw it work. She peeked at Liz from the corner of her eye. The girl startled whenever a nearby cow moved or swished her tail.

Jean leaned over and whispered to Liz. "Larry is our oldest son."

Liz nodded. "Oh, sure. He looks like Jim. How old is he?"

"He's nine."

"How many children do you have?"

"Three. There's Larry, Will is eight, and our youngest is James. He's six."

"Good grief! So close together!" Liz exhaled a light laugh and widened her eyes. "I can't even imagine." She waved a fly away from her face.

Tommy slipped through the crowd and joined them.

"What did you think?" he asked Liz. "Impressive, right?"

"It's swell," Liz said. She recoiled when a cow released a stream of urine in the stall next to them.

"Tommy, you'll never believe what happened earlier," Jean said, already smiling at the thought of telling him the latest Reverend Iverson hair flap. "I was dishing up food when—"

"What the hell are you wearing?" Tommy said, bending to examine the enormous boots on Liz's feet.

"You failed to mention that *shoes* would be required on a farm," Liz said.

"They still aren't." With that, he swooped her up and cradled her in his arms as she squealed and pulled down her skirt. The boots slid off her feet and landed next to Jean. Several men turned around to look, their interest in the milking machine momentarily interrupted.

"See?" Tommy said. "No shoes required." Liz laughed and tilted his baseball cap sideways.

"Jean, you'll put those boots away for me, right?" Tommy called as he carried Liz out of the barn.

"Sure," Jean said. She replaced the boots and followed.

Outside, Tommy was introducing Liz to Reverend Iverson. At the food table, Jean found her bowl of potato salad already empty. She cradled the crystal piece, her favorite because it had been a wedding gift from Tommy and she'd always loved the delicately etched rose pattern, in the crook of her arm and trudged across the yard. She stopped to pick up several discarded napkins. Jean took pride in their clean, tidy dairy operation—no junk piles or peeling paint on the buildings, with the exception of the old chicken coop behind her house, a rickety building with missing shingles and cracked windowpanes. It had evolved into a graveyard for broken tools and tractor parts, not to mention a haven for raccoons. Jean would just as soon burn it to the ground but Jim promised every spring to fix it up so she could park her Buick inside and not have to dig out of the snow and ice in winter. Many winters had passed, though, and she still had to plug the headbolt heater of her car into the outlet on the side of the house to ensure it would start from November to March.

At her front porch, Jean lowered herself onto the stoop to cool off in the shade and rest her aching feet from standing while she sliced vegetables and frosted cakes all morning.

A commotion stirred within the crowd at the edge of the yard. People milled about and moved into a circle with whistles for attention, shushes and shouts for quiet. Tommy and Liz stepped into the center, as if awaiting a stage performance. Jean spotted Jim and Bonnie standing in the innermost ring of the circle, behind Tommy. He raised his hands over his head and the crowd instantly hushed but for a single fussing baby—Mary Meyers' newborn girl, Jean easily recognized after trying to calm the child herself while volunteering in the nursery last Sunday.

"Now that I've got everyone's attention," Tommy said, "I have something important I want to say with all my family here by my side."

Jean stood, her arms still loaded with the bowl and trash, and moved closer to the outskirts of the crowd to hear better. No one moved to make room for her and she had to balance on her toes to see.

Tommy turned to Liz and gathered her hands into his own. "My old man, God rest his soul, used to tell me that when you know, you know."

He slowly lowered to one knee. A few women gasped and

covered their mouths.

Jean fought to keep her balance on her toes and the hard edges of the bowl dug into her ribs.

Tommy pulled a small ring from his front jeans pocket. "And right now, I just know. Elizabeth Belardi, will you marry me?"

Liz pressed her hands to her breasts, her eyes filling with tears. After a moment, she silently nodded.

"Is that a yes?" Tommy said.

She nodded again.

"She said yes!" Tommy shouted, and the crowd erupted into cheers.

Liz extended her visibly trembling left hand, tears streaming down her face, and Tommy stood to slip the ring onto her finger. When they finally kissed, he tipped her back into an elaborate dip as men tossed their hats into the air and cracked open cans of beer for a toast. The couple then embraced a jubilant Jim and Bonnie. No one seemed to notice Jean was missing from the family celebration.

Jean turned and walked away from the edge of the crowd, her legs heavy. She stumbled over the uneven terrain as she moved beyond the yard, dropping the dirty napkins from her hand one at a time. She followed a gravel lane behind the stanchion barn, past the silos and the hay barn, to a small slab of concrete used to hose down cattle behind the machine shed.

There, away from prying eyes, she hugged the crystal piece to her chest, feeling its heft and solid mass in her hands. Slowly, Jean raised the bowl over her head, as high as her arms would stretch, and hurled it against the concrete, shattering the crystal into a million sparkling shards. She dropped to her knees, shaking and breathless, momentarily shocked and remorseful at her impulsive action. She picked up a large fragment and turned it between her fingers.

After all this time, he was in love again.

With her family and neighbors still celebrating in her own front yard, Jean put the pointed tip of the crystal fragment to the tanned skin of her forearm, just below the elbow. She hadn't done this in many years, hadn't given in to the terrible, shameful urges in so long. But today she'd lost the strength to resist and broke her own promise. She pressed down on the glass and dragged it several inches, parting the flesh like the open mouth of a flour sack. She closed her eyes and held her breath for the pain and, simultaneously, the relief.

CHAPTER 2

August, 1963

Mornings, before the children awoke, Jean scrubbed her kitchen floor. She rose as soon as the alarm went off at 4:30 on her side of the bed and shook Jim's arm until he blearily sat up in his nightshirt and jockey shorts, and while he dressed for the morning milking, she went downstairs, started the coffee, and scrubbed her floor.

On her hands and knees, with the mixed aroma of dark roasted beans and lemon-scented soap, the rhythmic *shush shush shush* of stiff bristles across the linoleum lulled her into feeling like she was somehow wiping the slate clean from the previous day.

Once the floor was clean and the coffee brewed, she made an egg-and-toast sandwich that she took to Jim in the barn, along with a steaming mug of the coffee. He ate the sandwich in less than five bites while seated on his squat wooden milking stool, and drank the coffee in less than five gulps, somehow never scalding his mouth. If it was Tommy's week to work the morning shift, the coffee and egg sandwich were delivered to him. The morning routine was as reflexive and dependable to her as breathing, and Jean was never a woman to appreciate change or surprise.

With her morning routine complete, she was ready to move on to the next task. It was Thursday and her day for grocery shopping. For this trip to town, she took only Will and James while Larry was busy baling hay with Tommy.

She drove the eleven miles to Chickering in her white Buick wagon with the dented driver's door from Will's bicycle crash last summer, which had also resulted in his second broken bone in less than three years. Jean parked in front of Dawson's Drugstore, a business that not only shared space with a barbershop but also boasted The State's Largest Walleye ever caught and mounted.

On its best day, the city of Chickering, Wisconsin, was appealing enough to attract tired truckers off the highway for a bite to eat at the Little Chick Diner, or lure vacationing families overnight on their way to the Dells. The small-town feel was usually nice except on days like today, when Jean had many things to do and no time to get trapped by someone carrying on about so-and-so who did this-and-that, or worse, cornered into answering more questions about Tommy's engagement. The most likely place for this to happen was at Dawson's Drugstore with Alma Dawson herself, who Jean had been avoiding for the past month.

Jean unzipped her purse to retrieve the list Bonnie had sent in her masculine scrawl. *Hand cream, denture paste, nasal spray, Preparation H.* Bonnie never made a trip to the drugstore if any kind of intimate products were needed; she always recruited her only daughter-in-law for that job.

"Can I get a lollipop?" Will asked as he climbed out of the backseat and slammed the door behind him.

"Me too!" James held his chubby hand out for a coin.

"I suppose." Jean dropped the exact change into their sweaty palms and extracted a comb from her purse to give them each a quick groom with the help of a little spit. "But no comic books," she warned as they entered the store, a cowbell clanging over their heads.

Dawson's was busy today and there was a line at the counter. Howard Dawson was giving directions to Lake Koshkonong to a hopelessly lost young couple while several customers waited their turn, sweating and impatient. Jean quickly filled a basket and stepped to the back of the line, snapping her fingers at the boys when she caught them rough-housing in the aisle behind her.

"Mornin', Jean," Howard said, when it was her turn at the register. "Refill for Bonnie, right?"

"Yes, and some more of that antiseptic spray. Will has an infected mosquito bite on his leg that he won't stop scratching."

Will crossed his eyes at his mother at the mention of his own name.

"Stop it," Jean hissed under her breath. "Or your eyes will get stuck that way."

"Antiseptic, antiseptic..." Howard turned to the shelves behind him, reading the rows of labels with his bifocals held out several inches in front of him. Once again, he hadn't managed to knot the white apron tied about his waist so the strings dragged across the floor and turned the tips black, a fact that drove Jean crazy to no end.

"Well, good morning, Jean Krenshaw." Alma Dawson emerged from the storage room. "Haven't seen you in here for a while."

"Good morning, Alma," Jean said.

"I was just doing inventory," Alma said, wiping the back of her hand across her brow for effect.

Jean fought the urge to roll her eyes, knowing very well she hadn't been anywhere near the inventory. It was common knowledge that Alma Dawson spent most of her days sitting next to the telephone at the back of the storage room with her hand on the receiver waiting for it to vibrate, signaling a neighbor placing a call on the area party line. Alma would then snatch it up and listen in on the entire conversation.

"I hear Beverly is coming for a visit," Jean said politely.

"Next Sunday," Alma said. "And I can't wait to tell her the big news from your family. You all must be so excited!"

"Yes, the new milking machine is pretty exciting," Jean

answered.

"No, no! I meant the *wedding* news. Finally, that bachelor Tommy is getting married!"

"Oh, of course." Jean shook her head, feeling silly. She fanned herself with the Pennysaver from the counter. The metal handles of the heavy shopping basket pressed against the bandaged cut on her forearm beneath her long-sleeved shirt, and she could feel the tape loosening, pulling fine hairs with it, and the tender, healing flaps of the cut pried back open. She carefully lifted the handles and switched the basket to her opposite arm.

"How are you not more excited about this?" Alma said. "Jean Krenshaw, I swear you are the toughest nut to crack. So, what's she like?" Alma pressed. "Bonnie told me she's some famous artist from the city."

"Goodness, she's hardly famous," Jean said. "She takes art classes at the college."

"But gorgeous. I saw her at church on Sunday and she is breathtaking. I didn't get a chance to talk with her since I was in the choir." Alma suddenly took a step back and gave Jean a once over from head to toe. "Why on earth are you wearing a long-sleeved shirt? It's hot enough to fry eggs on the sidewalk out there!"

"William." Jean snapped again to her middle child. "Stop cracking your knuckles or you'll get arthritis before you're old enough to vote." She turned back to Alma, trying not to squirm under the woman's scrutiny.

"Anyway," Alma said. "Bonnie also told me that she's from Italy. Italy! Can you imagine? That sounds so *exotic.*"

As Alma's jaw flapped up and down in time with her hands, a black fly buzzed around her massive, stiff beehive, finally landing atop the mound of starched red hair. The insect scurried about for a moment before crawling down into the interior of the bouffant, becoming trapped in the sticky, Breck-sprayed cage. A closed mouth catches no flies, Jean's mother used to say. She suppressed a smile. A closed mouth catches no flies but apparently beehives do.

"Four eighty-six, Jean," Howard said. Jean handed him a five-dollar bill from her coin purse.

"Isn't it something to finally see him in love again," Alma said and clicked her tongue. "After that terrible tragedy with the Weaver girl so many years ago, I thought he'd never settle down. But look at him now!"

Jean's heart began to race at the mention of "the Weaver girl."

Sandy Weaver, a girl she rarely allowed herself to think about anymore.

She held out her now trembling hand to Howard, trying to hurry him along as he doggedly counted back her change. She shifted her purse straps further up her shoulder, feeling the adhesive of the bandage on her sweaty arm finally come loose.

Alma leaned closer and lowered her voice. "I know it was a painful incident for you, but I've always wondered if Tommy ever mentions Sandy anymore—"

"I should really be on my way," Jean cut her off. "I still need to stop at the grain elevator to drop an order off for Jim."

"Oh, well, don't let me keep you then." Alma sniffed and patted the sides of her hair, releasing the fly. "I should get back to work, myself."

"Alright, then," Jean said tightly and waved goodbye.

Outside, the boys ran down the sidewalk ahead of her. As she walked, Jean slowly rolled up her shirtsleeve. She ripped the last strip of tape from her arm and tossed the bandage onto the ground without missing a step.

*   *   *

During the drive home, Jean had a ridiculous moment of missing her mother. Ridiculous because she was really too old to experience this orphaned loneliness. But there it was anyway, that familiar longing for her mother to reach a hand down to the back of her head and draw her face into the folds of cloth at her thighs. That remembered smell of flour and brown sugar still made Jean want to bury her head in the kitchen canisters to this day whenever she felt upset.

At the outskirts of town, she suddenly took a detour and started heading straight east on a county road toward Cold Spring, the town where her mother was buried. Jean did this often, drove forty minutes out of her way to visit her mother's grave in the middle of the day. While Jim was unaware of the trips, her children were quite used to them, like stopping at the bank to make a deposit. They didn't even ask where they were going anymore as soon as she pointed the car east.

Once they reached the tiny Cold Spring cemetery, she parked the station wagon under a poplar tree and cut the engine.

"Boys," she said, craning her neck to face the backseat. James was fast asleep with his head cocked at a painful ninety-degree angle, a silvery string of saliva dangling from his lip. "William, I'll be just a minute, so wait here. And put your shoes back on," she added. "Your feet smell."

"Sorry," he said, tucking his feet beneath him. He propped his chin on his hand, studying a daddy longlegs spider walking along the sill of the open window.

Jean sighed and wiped dots of perspiration from her brow. "No, I'm sorry," she said. "I've been grumpy this week, I know."

William slid his gaze to her in the front seat and offered a small smile. "It's okay."

"How about I make some chocolate chip cookies when we get home?"

He returned to studying the bug and nodded. "Sure."

Jean exited the car and zigzagged through several rows to her mother's headstone, which stood out because of its unusual color—salmon pink marble. Jean knelt and pulled a few weeds that had sprouted since her last visit and straightened the silk roses in the vase on her mother's side, paying no notice to her father's neglected, undecorated side. She ran her fingers over the etched letters, *Hank M. "Toad" Gillman, Marjorie F. Sullivan Gillman, Parents of Marjorie Ann*. She picked off dried blades of grass that stuck to the face whenever the caretaker mowed.

Jean always remembered her mother with wet hands—from washing dishes in the sink, scrubbing buckets of potatoes and carrots, or wiping down windows and countertops with vinegar water. She used to give Jean sandwiches with damp bread, soppy dollar bills for the picture show or notes for the teacher—*Marjorie Ann missed school yesterday because she had a stomachache*—the inky handwriting smudged and running. But what Jean missed most was the sound of her mother's voice, soft and refined. She wondered how differently her life might have turned out had her mother lived, or if she'd had a sibling to talk with, someone to soften the loss.

Growing up, friends were hard to come by. They moved several times and were always poor. Jean was an easy target for teasing with her awkward height and bad teeth. As a constant outsider, she learned the art of observation and developed a keen understanding of female behavior. She subsequently handled members of her own sex with a distrusting arm's length regard.

Until Sandy Weaver, of course. And that had ended disastrously because Jean didn't keep her at arm's length. She should have known better.

Jean laid her head against the sun-warmed stone and tried to picture this new woman, this Liz, living in the matching house, just across the driveway. She closed her eyes and tried to imagine and instead dug the tip of her finger into the stinging cut on her arm.

It was the worm creatures in her blood again.

When Jean was thirteen, the same year her mother died, she contracted a deadly infection from a tick bite. For months, she'd suffered agonizing headaches, weakness and high fevers. The doctor who finally diagnosed the problem gently explained to her that she had parasites living inside her bloodstream. He showed her a picture of the hideous microscopic organisms with grotesque spindly-looking bodies and razor-sharp teeth.

Even though the doctor prescribed a dose of strong antibiotics and Jean eventually got better, she couldn't stop thinking about the picture in the doctor's medical journal of the worm-like creatures that had been swimming around inside her. She imagined them eating her alive from the inside out, nibbling away at her veins and organs, growing fatter and bigger on her tissue and organs. Her worry turned to obsession and she began to feel terrified, even convincing herself she could hear the worm creatures swishing through her bloodstream. One night, while preparing for bed, she took her father's razor from the medicine cabinet and, on an impulse, dragged it across the pale under skin of her forearm. The outpour of blood was instantaneous, welling up and running down her arm to her fingers in a thick crimson line. The pain was surprisingly delayed—two, three seconds—but when it did come in burning twinges, it felt oddly satisfying. She couldn't explain why she felt such an urge to do it, only that she wanted those nasty little worms to be carried away and outside of her body.

Long after she healed from the illness and stopped obsessing about the parasites, she would still cut herself—whenever school was difficult, or her father yelled at her, or the ache for her mother became unbearable. Each time she sliced into her skin, the feeling of pain always came with an equal feeling of relief. She continued the cutting until that last terrible night with Sandy, and then she'd vowed never to do it again. She would stop the cutting and punishing and atone for her sins. She promised herself. She promised God. And she kept her promise.

Until the picnic a month ago.

She reached into the front pocket of her shirt and removed the crystal fragment—all that was left of her beloved rose bowl, which she been carrying around with her for days. She held the fragment up to the sunlight for a moment, turning it left and right. She told Jim she'd sliced her arm on a barbed wire fence behind the barn when she threw a hay bale over for the cattle. He was concerned, told her to see Dr. Cleary for a tetanus shot, which she said she would.

The old lies and excuses for the cuts and burns rolled off her tongue so easily, even after all these years.

She pushed the shard into the soft ground at the base of the headstone, until the glass was completely hidden by the blades of grass.

Here, she would leave it and not be tempted again. Here, she would reaffirm her promises and not give in to the creatures in her blood.

CHAPTER 3

July 4, 1952

Jean Gillman hunched toward the steering wheel of her father's rattletrap truck, intensely concentrating on the gray snake of dry gravel road. She only received her license a few weeks before and was still a shaky driver, so when the truck began to fishtail on the loose rock, she slammed on the brakes and pulled to the shoulder. A covered bowl of potato salad slid off the bench seat onto the floorboards and a cloud of dust rolled through the open windows. Jean wrestled with the stubborn crank handle but failed to get the window completely up before a layer of grit settled on her hair and stung her eyes.

The truck shuddered and she gunned the ailing engine to keep it from dying. The pick-up surged back to life and she carefully steered onto the road, though slower this time.

"County road 51, county road 51," she muttered to herself, squinting at a faded metal sign. "One mile."

She was nervous. This would be her first time meeting anyone her own age since moving to Chickering a month ago and it was always an unpleasant process, no matter the town, no matter the people.

The truck banged along the county road as Jean was unable to avoid the numerous ruts and potholes. Finally, there it was, the Krenshaw Dairy, with its imposing barns and silos, nestled in the cleavage of two gently sloping hills.

Jean jerked on the steering wheel and sharply turned

the truck onto the driveway. She parked on the grass and shaded her eyes against the afternoon sun, trying to get a full view of the neighboring farm she'd been hearing her father gripe about for weeks. He had seen the Krenshaw's new John Deere 60 parked in front of the barn the day before—situated near the road so that every passerby had a full view of the fine machine—and he was not impressed.

Jean rubbed a smudge of dirt from the cuff of her pedal pushers and smoothed down the collar of her blouse. Her hair would frizz in the heat, never mind what the dust would do to it. She picked up her salad bowl and exited the truck.

As Jean walked across the yard, she took in the impressive gable-topped stanchion barn and pretty little matching farmhouses. There was already a large crowd assembled, friendly-looking people sitting on hay bales, balancing plates on their knees as they chatted and swatted the flies away. As she walked, Jean caught snippets of conversations. The men, with their sun-lined faces, worried over the fickle weather and fields too wet to cut, while the women gossiped in small huddles that so-and-so's husband was drinking again or so-and-so's daughter was caught in a parked car behind the city library last Saturday night with the windows fogged up. Jean could recite these conversations by heart. Same people, different place. Anywhere you hang your hat in Middle America.

"Jean! Over here!" a short, stout woman called from behind the food table. Bonnie Krenshaw, wife of the owner of the dairy. Jean waved.

"Good to see you again," Bonnie said, shaking Jean's hand.

"Thank you for inviting me," Jean said. "My father couldn't make it. He's with a laboring boar."

"Oh, too bad. I'm glad you could at least come. Make some friends your own age."

"It was very nice of you to invite me. I, I haven't met very many people yet."

"Mercy, you're tall," Bonnie said suddenly. She tilted her head up to look Jean over.

Jean felt her face turn red. "My father calls me the Jolly Green Giant."

Bonnie frowned. "I meant it as a compliment. Nothing wrong with being tall. You should tell your father that."

Jean pushed up her glasses, simultaneously flattered and apprehensive. "Here." She held out the covered bowl. "It's potato salad."

"Why, thank you. What a nice thing to do," Bonnie said, taking the bowl. "Your father told me you finished school last year."

"Yes, ma'am."

"Then you're Jim's age. He's our oldest. I should introduce you," Bonnie said. "He's somewhere out back making trouble with his brother."

"That would be great," Jean said.

"Walt and I live in that house there," Bonnie said, pointing to a small brown house a mile or so down the road. "His mother Beatrice lives there by herself." She pointed to the house on the west side of the driveway, then gestured to the matching house to the east. "And his Aunt Eunice lives in that one. They're both widows."

Jean had already heard about the famously inseparable twin Krenshaw sisters and their strange "twin ways." *Witches*, her father had called them.

Bonnie leaned in close and lowered her voice. "Bit of a crank, his Aunt Eunice, so I'd avoid her if I were you. Soon as she goes, we'll get Jim moved into her house. Eventually Tommy, our youngest, will get the other. He just graduated."

Jean nodded, but was stumped for a reply to such a disclosure.

Bonnie waved to a plump woman with a large rope of hair atop her head. "Beatrice!" she called. "Come meet Jean Gillman. She just moved over to Ellison's old hog farm with her father—what's his name again?"

"Hank," Jean said, "But everyone calls him Toad."

"He probably earned it," Bonnie muttered and started re-arranging the food table to make room for Jean's salad bowl.

"Hello, hello!" Beatrice cried and pulled Jean into a hug. Jean nearly cried out in pain when Beatrice unknowingly crushed the tender skin of her burned wrist.

"Now you can drop in anytime," Beatrice said, as if they were already mid-conversation. "We old ladies are always happy for visitors. And if you ever need anything, a ride to church on Sunday, just let me know. I should introduce you to my sister, Eunice." She tapped her finger against her bottom lip, craning her neck to look over the crowd. "She's probably on the porch, trying to get out of the sun. Oh!" She pressed Jean's hands, still cupped in her own, to her chest. "You have to meet my grandson, Jim. You're the same age. But first, let's get you something to eat. You need more meat on your bones."

She took Jean by the elbow and guided her straight to the end of the food table.

"You just moved here last month, is that right?" Beatrice asked, dropping spoonfuls of everything onto a plate.

"Yes, ma'am," Jean said. "From Helenville."

"So, it's just you and your father?"

Jean nodded. She accepted the overloaded plate of pork and beans, fruit salads of every color, sliced vegetables and a fat burger too big for the bun.

"Did your father raise hogs in Helenville too?" Beatrice asked.

"Uh, yes." Jean squirmed and bit into a crunchy, bitter slice of kohlrabi. She knew better than to talk about the hog farm in Helenville, about the mess with the bank and the foreclosure notices tacked to the door that Toad had ripped down and stomped with his boots. Unlike Bonnie, she would never share private family information with new neighbors.

Jean turned her attention to the crowd.

"So, it's just you and your father?" Beatrice pressed. "No farm hands right now?"

Jean shook her head. She noticed a group of young people milling about the barn looking in her direction, and her stomach tightened. Making good with old ladies was never a difficult part of settling into a new town. Making good with people her own age was another story.

"I, I could go inside and help with the food if you'd like," she said. She'd learned that putting herself to work in new places was the quickest way to blend in and not draw attention.

"Nonsense!" Beatrice said. "I want you to meet my grandson." She shielded her eyes and waved across the yard to the very group Jean had been hoping to avoid.

A lean boy wearing a bright Cubs baseball cap smiled and waved back from the open door of the hay barn where he'd been talking with a pretty blonde girl. As Jean watched him cross the lawn with a relaxed, unhurried stride, this Jim Krenshaw, he smiled at her. And oh, she couldn't tear her stare away from that smile. She hastily dumped the remainder of her plate in the garbage, licking her lips and brushing crumbs away from her chin. She regretted eating the kohlrabi, which always left her with bad breath.

"Over here," Beatrice called to him. "I want you to meet someone."

"Whatcha need, Grammy?" He put his grandmother in a headlock to give her a knuckle-rub.

"Just stop that!" She wrestled out of his grasp and smoothed down her hair. "Jean, this is my grandson, Tommy, the troublemaker of the two boys."

Jean felt the corners of her mouth drop in momentary confusion.

"Troublemaker?" Tommy protested, putting a playful fist up to his grandmother's jaw.

"Where's Jim? And where have you been all afternoon?"

"In the barn, trying to hide from Alma Dawson." He reached for a carrot. "She's determined to marry me off to her daughter and that Beverly is a *dog*."

Beatrice swatted the back of his head. "I'm trying to introduce you to Jean Gillman. She and her father just moved onto the Ellison's old hog farm."

"Oh, hey, then. Welcome to Chickering." Tommy smiled and playfully saluted her. "Always happy to add any female company to the neighborhood. And you're a helluva lot better looking than Beverly Dawson."

Jean blushed so furiously that beads of sweat broke out along the elastic of her brassiere, collecting, she could feel, at her sternum and sliding down between her breasts.

"I brought the potato salad," she said stupidly, pointing to her green bowl on the table.

Tommy turned to scan the army of bowls. "This one?" He pointed.

She nodded. He spooned a large helping onto a plate and took a bite while she watched.

"Ooooh, sweet Christ," he groaned, rolling his eyes. "This is fantastic!"

Jean laughed and covered her mouth.

"Thomas William Krenshaw! I'll wash your mouth out!" Beatrice cried.

He winked at Jean and the sweaty blushing instantly returned.

"Tommy, you should offer to help Jean's daddy out this summer," Beatrice said. "He doesn't have a farm hand right now. I'm sure your father can spare you for a few days."

Tommy shrugged. "Sure, Grammy, whatever you say."

"Did you know Jean and Jim are the same age?" Beatrice said. "Where is he, anyway?"

"Where's who?" a second boy asked, walking up behind Beatrice.

"Oh, Jim! We've been looking for you everywhere," Beatrice said. She linked her arm through his and pulled him to her side for a very obvious presentation that seemed to make him uncomfortable. He set his feet apart and held his seed corn logo cap in both hands, as if a soldier ordered to stand at attention.

"This is Jim, my other grandson I've been telling you about," Beatrice said. "Jim, this is Jean Gillman. She and her daddy just moved to the Ellison farm."

"Good to meet you," he said, extending a stiff arm. The hard and callused skin of his palm rubbed against her own. He wiped a film of sweat from his brow with a red handkerchief from his back pocket and replaced his hat. They stood in awkward silence. He was certainly not unhandsome, Jean decided, but next to his brother, it was a rather unfair comparison.

"You play horseshoes?" Jim asked. "We've got a pit set up behind my grandmother's house." His voice and expression were serious.

Jean wiped away a small pool of perspiration at the base of her throat. "Um, I—" Her gaze skipped back and forth between the brothers.

"Finally!" Beatrice cried. "Here's my sister, Eunice."

A small, thin woman wearing a flowered housedress shuffled toward the group, her movements slow.

"Eunice, this is—"

"I know who she is," Eunice said. She slapped a mosquito and killed it on her forearm. "How could I not know what with you squawking about every little goings-on up and down the road every five minutes?" She flicked the mosquito away and wiped at the dark smear on her skin with a tissue from her pocket.

"Oh," Beatrice scoffed, "put away your vinegar and welcome the poor girl to the neighborhood."

Eunice ignored her sister. "Where have you been?" she

asked Tommy. "You were supposed to bring me something to drink."

"I've been out back smooching with the preacher's wife, Aunt Eunie." Tommy smirked, and Jim elbowed him in the ribs.

"You just hush it." Eunice stuck a long, bony finger under his nose.

"For Heaven's sake," Beatrice said. "I'll get your drink." She waddled off to the food table.

Several teenagers wandered over to the group and started talking with Jim and Tommy. Eunice walked away and settled back into a rocking chair on the porch. Ignored and left standing alone, Jean stared down at her dingy canvas shoes. The laces were stained and yellowed, no matter how many times she bleached them. She hated those shoes. She wished she could've worn a nice summer dress with a pair of sandals, something prettier, more feminine. The group chattered on without her, bantering around unfamiliar names and references. Their voices swirled and overlapped in a way that made her feel invisible, like a shrub they had merely congregated next to.

Tommy caught her eye. "You never said whether or not you play horseshoes," he said. He plucked a blade of grass to chew.

"Oh, just a little." Her voice sounded high-strung.

"So, it's just you and your dad, I gather?"

"Yes. I'm an only child. My mother died of cancer when I was thirteen." She blanched at the added comment about her mother. She normally didn't talk about Marjorie.

"It must be tough," he said, "being new in town, trying to make friends."

Jean nodded, surprised by the hard lump forming in her throat. No one had ever acknowledged the struggle to start over somewhere new, or even cared. She wiped the back of her hand across her sweaty brow.

Tommy caught Jean's fingers and held them between his own. A breath snagged in her chest at the unexpected skin-to-skin contact.

"What happened here?" he said, looking at her burned wrist.

She jerked her hand away and rolled her long-sleeved shirt back down and buttoned the cuff. "I burned it, on accident. On a teapot."

The previous night, unable to sleep in her agitated state, she'd impulsively pressed the edge of a hot teakettle to her arm, leaving an angry red arc on the thin skin of her inner left wrist. But she promised herself that was the last time and that she would stop all that nonsense now that they were in Chickering. She would make a fresh start.

Tommy studied her face, his expression serious.

"I...it's fine. Really. I'm very clumsy." Jean moved the grass around with the toe of her shoe. She wished he would stop looking at her with that doubting, yet sympathetic face. She'd never been around a boy who made her feel so undone.

"Think you could still play that game of horseshoes?"

She exhaled a relieved breath. "Sure."

Beatrice returned after delivering Eunice's iced tea. "Are you having a good time, Jean?" she asked.

"Yes, thank you. Actually, we were just going to play some horseshoes."

"What an excellent idea!" Beatrice said. "Jim, I need you over here." She cupped one hand around her mouth in a dramatic whisper directed at Tommy. "You know, Jean's the same age as Jim and I've already set to working on them."

"You need something, Grammy?" Jim asked.

"Yes, take Jean and go play a game of horseshoes." She took a glass out of his hand and nudged him in Jean's direction.

"Okay." Jim offered her his elbow.

Tommy grinned at them both and punched his brother in

the forearm. "You kids have fun." He pointed at Jean. "And bring around more of that potato salad sometime!"

"But, I—" Jean started to say.

"Jim, get her something to drink first," Beatrice said. "It's so hot out here."

"Whatever you say, Grammy." Jim looked at Jean and shrugged his shoulders with a just-do-what-I'm-told expression.

Jean followed Jim back to the food table where he poured her a cup of tea from a large glass pickle jar.

"How's the farm so far?" Jim asked.

"Fine," Jean said.

They stood in silence for a moment and Jean sipped her tea.

"It's a dry one this summer," Jim finally said. "Does your father have any crops?"

"Corn and soybeans," she said.

"Hmm." He shoved his hands into his pockets.

Jean's gaze drifted across the yard to where Tommy was talking with the group of young people, the pretty blonde again.

"If you ever want a ride to church on Sunday I can pick you up," Jim said.

"Thanks. That's nice of you to offer."

"Chickering United Methodist," he said. "Good choir."

"Hmm." Jean nodded. She finished her tea and threw the empty cup away.

"How about that game of horseshoes now?" Jim said.

"Okay," Jean said and followed him to the horseshoe pit.

They played three games—best of two—with few words exchanged. After Jean won the third and final game, Jim shook her hand as if they'd just brokered a sale price on livestock. Jean excused herself to sit in the shade and they politely parted company.

She joined Eunice on the porch.

"Is this seat taken?" Jean asked, gesturing to another rocking chair.

"You're welcome to it," Eunice said, fanning herself with a paper plate.

Jean sat down. "It's nice here in the shade."

The old woman didn't respond and continued to fan herself. She closed her eyes and leaned her head back. Jean clasped her hands in her lap and wondered how long she had to stay before she could leave without appearing rude.

She noticed a low, steady hum then, and looked around the porch. She quickly spotted a football-shaped paper nest hanging from a branch of the tree next to the eaves. Dozens of bald-faced hornets crawled around the opening at the bottom.

"There's a hornet's nest," Jean said, pointing.

Eunice opened her eyes and stopped fanning herself. "Yes," she said. "My nephew was supposed to knock it down before the party but he didn't get around to it."

"Should we move?" Jean asked.

"They won't bother you if you don't bother them."

Jean warily eyed the buzzing nest. "I was stung by a hornet once. So painful."

"I'm allergic to hornets," Eunice said. "Nearly died from a sting when I was a child."

"Really?"

Eunice nodded. "Beatrice saved my life. She treated it with a special poultice she made—whiskey and ammonia. Then she soaked me in tubs of ice water."

"And it worked?"

"I'm still here, aren't I?" Eunice said. She leaned her head back once more and started rocking the chair. "People thought she'd used witchcraft. They thought we had demonic powers, that we could read people's minds and predict the future. Change the weather. Speak to animals. Our mother finally had to school us at home."

Jean studied the old woman's angular face. "That's terrible," she said quietly.

Eunice shrugged. "I didn't care what they thought."

Tommy and the group of young people burst into laughter.

"I like your nephews," Jean said, watching them from afar. "Tommy told Beatrice he would help my father on the farm a little this summer. That was very generous of him." She was smiling as she spoke and when she turned back to Eunice to say something more, she was startled to see the old woman staring hard at her.

"Tommy only likes a certain kind of girl," Eunice said.

"Oh, I, I..."

Eunice leaned onto the armrest of the rocker. "It's a difficult life to live so close to what you cannot have. Remember that, Jean Gillman."

Jean shrank from Eunice's unnerving, rheumy stare. "I don't understand what...you mean," she said.

The branches high in the tree above them began to rustle, raining bits of leaves and twigs onto the ground and porch roof. Jean and Eunice looked up and a white barn owl, with its heart-shaped face and black eyes, peered down at them from its perch.

"White owl in daylight," Eunice said, her eyes widening. "It's a bad omen."

"What?"

Eunice clamped her hand on Jean's arm and Jean jumped. Eunice's fingers were sharp and curled like the claw of a hawk, and she pulled Jean close.

"Curses, like chickens, come home to roost," she whispered, her breath hot against Jean's ear.

Jean yanked her arm away and recoiled from the old woman. As she stood, preparing to leave, the owl suddenly released a piercing screech and made a graceful dive from the high branch, swooping through the porch in a silent, ghostly flight. Jean gasped and ducked her head. The owl made a second pass and its massive wing brushed the side of the paper nest. A swarm of angry hornets poured from the opening and instantly surrounded Jean and Eunice like a dark cloud.

Jean cried out and swatted at the raging insects. She stumbled down the steps of the porch and ran across the yard, one hornet stinging the back of her neck. As she turned around to look back over her shoulder, she saw Eunice still on the porch, frantically batting at dozens of hornets attacking her arms and face until she collapsed, unmoving, onto the floor.

CHAPTER 4

October, 1963

Of the twin sisters who'd built the matching farmhouses decades ago, it was Eunice who had previously occupied Jean's house. Even though it was Jim's grandmother Beatrice who Jean had known so well, it was Eunice who Jean felt most connected to. Over the years, Jean had found random items left behind by the notoriously private woman: a pearl button under the old ice box in the kitchen, a pink hair comb on a shelf in the pantry, a bright blue stain on the hardwood floor of the master bedroom, discovered after the carpet had been pulled up, and a steamer trunk in the attic full of random keepsakes someone had carefully wrapped, stored and forgotten about, leaving behind an unintended inheritance.

Jean could still feel the old woman's claw-like grasp on her arm, and the breath of those final, haunting words against her ear. She never told Jim or anyone else about what Eunice said to her that day on the porch, but those brief moments alone with Eunice still spooked her, like a ghost that appeared every now and then to rattle its chains and roam the house, lest it be forgotten.

After the news of the engagement died down, Jean spent the remainder of the summer and fall throwing herself into the usual household chores, those familiar tasks that normally kept her hands and mind occupied. She moved about her kitchen with robotic efficiency preparing a breakfast plate and mug of coffee for Tommy.

At the end of the month, Liz would move in with Tommy, and the couple would be married.

It's a difficult life to live so close to what you cannot have. Remember that, Jean Gillman.

Ever since the engagement announcement, Eunice's words had started replaying in her head.

Jean tucked an empty milk jug under her free arm and walked a path between the houses worn down to bare dirt by a thousand footsteps. She stopped at the cattle lot to read the ear tag of a cow in heat, the large heifer trying to mount the back of another. With the number memorized, Jean moved on. She approached the line of lighted windows, the only lights on the farm at this early morning hour, and heaved open a side door of the stanchion barn. A swallow fluttered overhead and found a new perch high in the rafters.

Tommy smiled at her from where he sat hunched over on the milking stool in a stall, suctioning the four stainless steel milkers to a restless heifer's long pink teats.

"Hey!" he called over the hum of the equipment. "Mastitis, number 621. Write it on the board for Jim to treat when he milks tonight."

Jean stepped into the milk house and set the food down on a shelf below a blackboard.

"I'm starving," Tommy said behind her. He untied his rubber apron and washed his hands in the small basin, and took a generous bite of the sandwich.

"Five twenty-nine is in heat," Jean said.

"I know. Add four forty-one to the board, too. They'll both need bred today."

Jean jotted the numbers down on the blackboard.

"Jim's still planning to come to Madison with me on the 28th, right? I can't move that piano by myself."

"Yes, of course," Jean said, fussing with the chalk in the tray. "The boys and I will milk the morning shift that day."

"You're a gem." Tommy gently chucked her under the

chin with his fist.

Jean removed the lid to the empty milk jug and squatted down in front of one end of the bulk tank. She pulled on a small valve handle and released a stream of milk, watching the slow rise of bubbles as the jug filled.

"Say, Jean, I want to ask you something," Tommy said. "Were you nervous about marrying Jim?"

A ripple passed through Jean's stomach. She *knew* it. She knew it. She'd designed his words in her head a thousand times in the months since the picnic—*I'm having second thoughts. We rushed into the engagement. Liz isn't suited for life on a dairy farm. We're just too different*—and carefully constructed her answers and how she would approach them.

Jean took her time answering, scraping the layer of bubbles from the top of the jug with the lid. "I don't recall feeling nervous. Why?"

Tommy shifted from one foot to the other. "Oh, just, you know…"

"Is something wrong?"

"No, well, I don't know." He raked his fingers through his hair and turned to the blackboard. He picked up a piece of chalk and traced the numbers Jean had written just moments before, following the neat, confident curves of her six and two.

"Are you worried about how different you and Liz are?" she asked. "Is that it?" She really wanted to say—*apple pie and cannoli do not make a marriage.*

When he didn't answer, she continued. "Or are you just worried about marriage in general?"

"I'm not worried about getting married," he said quickly, dropping the chalk. "Or about any differences with Liz."

Jean looked up at her own reflection, warped and ugly, in the wavy steel of the tank. "Then, what is it?"

"What if Liz doesn't tell me everything…like what happened with Sandy."

Milk overflowed the top of the jug and spilled onto the concrete floor. Jean jammed the valve shut and shook the white droplets from her hands. She stood and turned around.

"I can't go through something like that again," he said.

Jean started to turn away at the mention of Sandy's name. She couldn't seem to get away from her these days.

"Jean," Tommy said, grasping her shoulders. "You have to help me. I mean, you have to help Liz. She's a city girl and never lived on a farm. She could really use someone to help her get adjusted."

Jean was shaking her head before he even finished. "Oh, I, I don't—" She cleared her throat. "I don't know her well enough…"

"Sandy was so fond of you," he said. "You were such a good friend to her, and I just thought maybe you could, you know, do the same for Liz. Get to know her better."

Jean's gaze wandered to the east window and she squinted against the strengthening light of the sunrise. Again, the image of Sandy's fair hair fanned out across the backseat of the cab flashed through her mind. Goose pimples broke out across the skin of her forearms and the back of her neck and she felt an overwhelming urge to claw away her own skin.

Jean looked back at Tommy's face, his pleading eyes, his needy, sincere expression, and she softened. She'd never been able to deny him anything he asked of her.

"Of course," she said. "Of course, I'll help her."

"I knew you would." Tommy exhaled a relieved sigh and pulled her against his chest, his arms tight around her shoulders and hands pressed against her back. His cotton t-shirt smelled conversely of sweet fabric softener and iodine.

Jean closed her eyes and leaned deeper into him. The troubling memory from moments before began to dissolve.

"You're the best," he said. "I don't know what I'd do without you."

They started to sway slightly, the first warm tips of sunlight brushing the tops of their heads, and Jean felt as if she were falling into a bed of clouds and wished the sensation could last forever. But almost as soon as the embrace had begun, he released her and moved away. He picked up his sandwich and resumed eating as if there had been no interruption to his meal.

"I can't believe how hungry I am this morning," he said, shaking his head.

Jean stared at him unblinking. The sun was now a full, fiery ball in the window, piercing her eyes until they watered and blinked of their own will. She turned back to the milk jug on the floor, her vision swirling with the sting of tears and embarrassment.

"Is Liz apprehensive about moving to a farm?" Jean finally asked, her voice flat but steady as she screwed the lid onto the jug.

"Yeah, a little." Tommy tried to laugh but it sounded forced. "But she's also trying to pack her apartment, get the wedding planned and all that. You know how she gets when she's stressed."

"Oh, sure," Jean said, even though she didn't know how Liz got when she was stressed, because she didn't know this Liz at all.

Tommy slid the apron back over his head and opened the door to the main barn. "This is gonna be great when Liz gets here. We'll have the Three Musketeers again."

He slipped through the door and it banged shut behind him. Jean turned back to the fire in the window and shuddered.

CHAPTER 5

August, 1952

Mornings, before her father awoke and while it was still dark, Jean Gillman scrubbed the kitchen floor. Even though the checkerboard linoleum was curling at the edges and worn through in the most-used places—in front of the sink and stove—she still started her day on her hands and knees with a bucket of hot soapy water.

It was the smell. Hog manure. She couldn't stand the embarrassing odor that permeated their house, clothes, and shoes. Sometimes it even clung to her hair and skin and she hated it. She hated the hogs and sloppy, run-down lots. She hated the sagging house, peeling paint, and the tiny, dingy rooms. But she could keep a clean kitchen floor. That much she could do.

It had been one month since the Fourth of July picnic. One month, but for Jean, a lifetime had come to pass.

After Eunice's shocking death from the hornet stings, the Krenshaws fully embraced her. She was personally invited by Beatrice to sit with the family at the funeral, asked by Bonnie to help at the luncheon reception afterward, and twice rode to Sunday church services with Jim. Even though she didn't like to think of it in such an unflattering light, Eunice's loss had become Jean's gain.

And Tommy kept his promise to his grandmother. He'd been helping Jean's father out several days a week.

Jean's movements were light and buoyant as she scrubbed

the floor beneath the kitchen table, pausing for a moment to rub a smudge of dirt off a rusted metal chair leg. She couldn't get Tommy's smile out of her head, the curve of his full, berry-colored lips, or the sound of his laugh. She felt out of sorts just thinking about it, and she knocked her head on the corner of the table as she crawled out from underneath.

Her daydreams about him were like a captured firefly; each time she opened her cupped hands just an inch to take a peek, the bug was off, flashing and flying about the yard, needing to be chased down. It was ridiculous, her distraction. She had too many things to do today. Laundry to hang. Windows to wash. A garden to weed. Yesterday she'd discovered an outbreak of crabgrass popping up in her cucumber patch. It was important to make herself useful around her father's house. She was an extra mouth to feed. Now was not the time for daydreams.

Jean's father stirred from his bedroom down the hall, slow to wake. The bedsprings squealed as he rolled from side to side with intermittent deep-lung coughs. She quickly began to prepare two eggs, two strips of bacon and a bowl of oatmeal for him, just the way her mother had taught her.

Marjorie Gillman had died one week after Jean's thirteenth birthday, and Jean had been left alone with her father's crushing grief from which he never fully recovered. While other girls her age were learning to cook and sew under the watchful eyes of their mothers, Jean was already preparing meals and running a household entirely on her own. She took to a needle and thread and found her way around a kitchen out of necessity.

Despite being an unsupervised teen, left alone during the most wilding hours of the day, Jean had avoided getting herself into any sort of adolescent trouble. She could've taken up smoking, or sneaked sips from her father's whisky bottles, or landed in the backseat of a car with a boy, but she'd been too occupied with the business of survival. A grown-up long before she was an adult.

Jean lit a burner on the stove to melt a spoonful of lard for the bacon, the way Toad liked it. She remembered a time when her father was happy, when he was still known as Hank and whistled "Down in the Valley" every night when he scrubbed his hands for dinner. How he'd carried her on his shoulders around the county fair when she got too tired to walk, and took her to Bud's soda fountain in town for her first root beer float on her ninth birthday. How she once stood on the seat of the truck next to her mother with her arm wrapped around Toad's neck—she would've been four, maybe five years old—as he drove them to some lake where they sat on a dock with their bare feet dangling in the water. She remembered what he was like before his cough, caused by the early years he spent working as a stone cutter up north when he inhaled massive clouds of thick, gritty dust while also smoking two packs of cigarettes a day.

Jean set a pot of water on to boil for her father's poached eggs.

"Something's burning," Toad said as he entered the kitchen, sniffing the air.

The lard had scorched in the frying pan, sending up a small, unpleasant curl of dark smoke.

"Oh!" Jean snatched the pan off the burner and rinsed it in the sink. The cool water hissed against the hot cast iron.

"Pay attention," Toad said. He shook his head and sat down. The stub of a Winston Red smoldered down to the hardened skin of his thumb and index finger, but he seemed not to notice. He coughed—a single, crackling explosion that bounced him up from the chair. He pressed a dingy handkerchief to his mouth to catch the tar-like phlegm his rotten lungs regularly ejected, and wheezed.

Jean set a cup of black coffee in front of him. She switched on the small radio atop the icebox to the morning farm report and cracked open the eggs over the boiling pot of water.

She scraped another spoonful of lard into the pan along with strips of bacon, and a greasy bubble popped and splattered her hand. She jerked away in pain but made no sound. She switched on the tap and thrust her hand under the cool water to ease the sting.

"That Krenshaw boy's comin' again today to help feed the hogs," Toad said.

Jean's heart leaped up to the back of her throat. She patted her hand with a dry dishcloth.

"What time?" she tried to ask casually. She set his breakfast plate on the table.

Toad sliced his eggs in half. "In about an hour. You'll have to feed him lunch again." He pointed at her with his fork. "And I don't trust him so keep an eye out. He fools around too much and drives the tractors too fast. He's reckless, that one."

A watched pot never boils, Jean's mother used to say, and Jean had never felt the truth of those words more than in the hours before lunchtimes with Tommy. She baked a glazed apple crisp, sliced ham, cheese and lettuce for sandwiches, and made a bowl of potato salad. She combed her hair and changed into a pretty plaid shirt.

Finally, it was noon and Tommy appeared at the screen door wearing a white T-shirt, dusty blue jeans and the smile.

"Hey, there," he said. "Your father said to just come on in. He's still on the tractor."

"Of course," Jean said. "Come in."

Tommy took off his ball cap and brushed his damp hair from his brow.

"It'll just take me a minute to fix your sandwich." Jean removed the ham, cheese, lettuce, and salad from the icebox.

"No hurry," Tommy said. "Sweet Christ, it's hot today!"

Jean checked the outdoor temperature gauge wired to the screen window. "Ninety-eight in the shade."

He whistled through his teeth. "Ninety-eight. How can

you stand to wear long sleeves?"

"I wish it would rain," Jean said, changing the subject. She set a plate of food in front of him. "My garden is withering."

"Milk production is always lower when it's hot," Tommy said, biting into the sandwich. "We got sprinklers running all day to keep the cattle cool."

She poured him a glass of iced tea into a plastic tumbler and added a mint leaf she'd picked from her garden that morning. She sat down in the chair next to him.

Tommy looked around. "Jean Gillman, I swear I could eat off your floor. I've never seen a house so clean!"

"You say that every time you come here," she laughed.

"Well, some day I'm gonna do it. I'm gonna *literally* eat off your floor just to prove my point."

A warm knot formed in the pit of her stomach at his compliment. It was Tommy's teasing that Jean liked best about him. Poking fun at her meticulous housekeeping, his faked exasperation when she wouldn't let him help in the kitchen, pretending to find a hair or a bug in his sandwich and then laughing at her horrified reaction. Even when it embarrassed her and made her face turn hot, she still enjoyed it. The feeling of his attention reminded her of how she'd felt when her mother had laughed, like stepping outside into the unexpected spring sunshine for the first time after a long stretch of dismal winter days.

"Before I forget," she said, and slid a small newspaper bundle across the table to him. "Just a little something I made for you."

"For me?" he said.

"It's nothing much."

He wiped his hands together and tore the paper apart. Inside was a simple button up work shirt she'd sewn for him out of some extra blue material she had on hand, material that reminded her of the sky blue color of his eyes.

He unfolded the shirt and held it up. "This is really swell," he said. "You didn't have to go to all that trouble."

"It wasn't any trouble. I had some extra material and didn't want it to go to waste. You said last week you tore your shirt on a barbed wire fence."

"That's nice of you. Thanks," Tommy said. "Say, I've been meaning to tell you that there's a Labor Day potluck at the church next week. You should come with us."

Jean grinned so hard she thought her cheeks would split. "I would love to."

He held his gift up beneath his chin. "And I'll wear my new shirt!"

CHAPTER 6

November, 1963

Larry backed the loaded half-ton Chevy up to the house as Tommy supervised from the porch steps, gesturing *closer, closer, stop!* Jean had caught the boy driving the truck around the farm several times over the summer even though she had forbidden him, and knew full well it was Tommy encouraging it behind her back, reckless as he could sometimes be.

Will and James waited on the porch with Liz, anxious to be handed a box or a lamp, something to lift and make them part of the excitement. It wasn't every day that someone new came to live on the farm. The boys had been antsy during breakfast and needed prodding to finish their eggs before they could go outside to wait for their father and uncle to return from Madison.

Tommy released the tailgate and untied the rope and twine securing the heaviest pieces of Liz's furniture—a newly-upholstered sofa, a rocking chair, an antique vanity table, and her upright piano. Not to mention endless stacks of cardboard boxes.

Jean approached the truck with a determined smile.

"Jean!" Tommy yelled. "Grab this couch before I break my back!"

Jean ran to the tipping end of the sofa, which was perilously close to sliding off the tail of the truck onto Tommy's toes.

"This is heavier than it looks," he grunted from the opposite end.

"It's a sofa-sleeper," Liz said. She balanced a box on her hip and held the front door open as wide as it would go so they could shove the sofa through.

"How the heck did you get it into the truck to begin with?" Jean asked, once the sofa was safely on the ground.

"One of Liz's neighbors took pity on us," Tommy said.

"Who's going to help you here?" Liz set the box on the counter and smoothed some flyaway strands of hair off her face.

"I'll help," Larry said from the doorway, crossing his arms over his chest and standing a little taller.

"Sure you can, Sport." Tommy pulled him into a head-lock. "And then you can drive these empty casserole dishes over to Grandma Bonnie's house later." He smiled and tossed a piece of wadded newspaper at Jean's head. She feigned a dirty look.

Jim emerged from the bedroom carrying a large box, his face red from the strain.

"Where do you want this one, Tommy?" he asked. James was not far behind, dragging a sack across the floor.

"Oh, Jim, that one's full of books," Liz said. "Don't hurt yourself."

"Just put it down right here," Jean ordered, "before you give yourself a hernia."

"It's not that bad." He dropped the box onto the floor with a smack and went back outside.

Liz tossed her long braid over her shoulder and Jean caught a glimpse of smooth, dark skin through the open laces of Liz's white peasant top. She obviously wore no brassiere underneath. The faint outline of her nipples pressed against the cotton material made Jean blush and she looked away in uncomfortable embarrassment. She'd never in all her life seen another woman deliberately walk out in public with nipples showing for all of God and mankind to see. Not only was it shocking, it was downright disturbing, like they were constantly staring at her.

Jean refocused on unpacking the boxes of books quickly overtaking the house. She glanced at the covers as she removed each one—art books, photography books, biographies of Susan B. Anthony and Elizabeth Cady Stanton.

"Goodness! So many," she said. "I wish I had time to read." She punctuated the statement with an exaggerated sigh.

"I *make* time to read," Liz said.

Jean stiffened. "Oh, sure, I meant, I should try and read more..." She tried to explain, but became too tongue-tied to finish.

Liz ignored her and slid a book out from the bottom of the pile and thrust it at Jean. "This one is a masterpiece."

Jean tilted her head and read the title on the spine aloud. "*The Feminine Mystique.*"

"One of my professors gave it to me." Liz tapped the cover. "It exposes suburbia as a bedroom and kitchen sexual ghetto."

Jean glanced around the room, eager to change the subject. She'd been around these new feminist women before, like Mary Meyers from church. Two years ago Mary had moved to Chicago to sing with some jazz band, but barely a month after arriving in the Windy City, she met George Meyers at a club where she was performing, fell madly in love, eloped, immediately got pregnant, and moved back to Chickering so George could work in her father's plumbing business. Now, whenever she brought her screaming newborn to the church nursery, she talked endlessly to Jean about how she had her own apartment in Chicago, how she fought a bank to let her open her own checking account without her father's signature, and how she marched in the 1961 Women Strike for Peace anti-nuclear weapons movement in Washington, D.C. with Dagmar Wilson. Jean had been wholly unimpressed because she hadn't a clue who Dagmar Wilson was and had already been told by Alma Dawson that when Mary moved to Chickering, George opened their checking account and Mary's name wasn't on it. As far as Jean was concerned, Mary Meyers could march from here to the moon, but she still had to ask for grocery money from her husband every week just like everyone else around here, and Liz would end up doing the same, no matter how many books she read.

Jean held up a red clay bowl, the glaze coating as smooth and perfect as a pane of glass. "Did you make this?" she asked.

"Mm-hmm," Liz answered. "And those figurines by the window."

Jean stood and walked around the table in front of the picture window, gently brushing her fingers over the shiny surfaces. The simple familiarity of Tommy's house was fading with each new box Liz opened. Empty end tables were now cluttered with pottery and knickknacks. There were throw pillows and blankets with strange abstract designs draped over the back of the sofa and lounge chairs. Tommy's prized stuffed deer head had been moved from the mantle and replaced by an enormous canvas painting of a naked woman's blue silhouette. Jean had the urge to toss her coat over it every time her children entered the room.

"This is nice." She gestured to a slender vase.

"Thanks," Liz replied and ran a dust rag over the top of the coffee table. She paused. "So, tell me something about yourself, Jean. We're about to be family."

Jean's hand fluttered to her chest at the word *family*, a notion that still felt shocking and foreign. "Something about myself. Like what?"

Liz returned to dusting as she talked. "Like, when did you and Jim get married?"

Jean followed her around the room. "Oh, early March. Between the planting and harvest season."

"That doesn't sound very romantic!" Liz laughed.

Jean pushed her glasses up her nose and tried to mask her annoyance. Liz's little comments somehow made her feel inadequate. Like the comment she'd made at the picnic about how close Jean's children were in ages.

"Where does this one go?" Jean asked, holding up a small shoebox.

"Um, bathroom," Liz answered. "It's all my toiletries. You can just shove them under the sink for now."

Jean escaped, relieved to get away. She switched on the light above the medicine cabinet and went to work setting the bottles of shampoo, hairspray and oils—occasionally flipping open a lid to sniff the contents—in a line under the dripping pipes of the sink next to Tommy's few personal items. At the bottom of the box, Jean found a small pink container, flat like a compact. She popped the lid. Inside were rows of tiny colored pills labeled by the day of the week. After several seconds, Jean realized what they were. Birth control pills. She'd never seen them in person, let alone known a woman who actually used them.

"Jean, we should—" Liz said behind her and Jean jumped.

"Oh! I, I'm so sorry." She hastily snapped the lid shut and stupidly held the container out to Liz.

Liz stared at the pink box for a moment before taking it.

"I'm not a slut," she finally said, fixing her stare on Jean.

"Liz, I really am sorry. I was unpacking and—"

"He doesn't know," she said, turning the container over in her hands.

Jean stood and nervously perched on the edge of the sink. "Know what?"

"That I...take them."

The screen door clapped again and Tommy yelled for Liz to take a box of clothes to the bedroom.

Liz quickly slipped the container into the pocket of her skirt. "I would appreciate it if you didn't say anything to him," she said. "He talks about having kids all the time and I, you know, would like to wait a while." She stepped into the hallway and lit a cigarette. "I just don't know if I could handle a baby right now, getting used to a new husband and house."

Jean was surprised by Liz's unexpected display of vulnerability and honesty. She recalled only too well her own early days on the farm, lonely and isolated but carrying on. And yet, she thought of Tommy's worry not long ago in the milk house, that Liz would keep secrets from him, and Jean's promise to befriend her and help her adjust.

"It's not always easy here," Jean said quietly. "But you get used to it. And this is something you should probably talk to Tommy—"

The screen door squealed open and Tommy yelled for Liz once again. She hurried back into the living room.

"I'm here!" She called and ran to Tommy. "What do you think so far? About the house?" She crushed out her cigarette in an ashtray shaped like a giant palm leaf.

Tommy stopped and planted his hands on his hips with a grin that Jean recognized would be followed by a tease. "It looks...like a flea market."

"What? You rat!" Liz swatted his arm.

"I'm just joking!" Tommy laughed, and Liz affixed herself his side, like a tightly screwed nut to a bolt.

Jean moved into the kitchen, her unspoken words still itching the back of her throat.

Jim and the boys entered and began to gather empty boxes to burn in the back yard.

"Hey, Liz," Will said. "Knock, knock."

Liz smiled. "Who's there?"

"Cow go."

"Cow go who?"

"No, silly, cows go moo!" Will erupted into a fit of laughter and James quickly followed.

Jean had a private habit of classifying people as inanimate objects, and if her children were fruit, Larry would be a breakfast orange, basic and common, James would be a plum, sweet and delicious, and Will would be a bright yellow banana. She had always found something mildly vulgar about bananas.

"Why do elephants paint their toenails?" James asked.

Liz shook her head and laughed again. "I don't know. Why do elephants paint their toenails?"

"So they can hide in a strawberry patch." He laughed and slapped his knee.

"You told it wrong, stupid," Will said. "It's why do elephants paint their toenails *red*."

"Shut up!" James blushed and punched his brother in the shoulder. The two tussled briefly in a wrestling match before Tommy twisted up a kitchen towel and tauntingly waved it over their heads. Liz stepped in to defend them. He snapped the towel at her rear in response and the boys burst into another fit of laughter. Jim then wound up a second towel and joined.

"Both of you, stop!" Liz squealed in a girlish, singsong voice. "*Taw*-mee!" There was not even a trace of the serious conversation she'd been having just moments before. Jean could see the faint outline of the pill container in Liz's pocket.

Jean slipped on her coat and gathered a pile of flattened boxes. "Do these need to be burned?" she asked over the commotion. "Hello? Do these need to go out to the burn pile?"

But no one was listening. No one even looked in her direction. It struck Jean, then, that every male in the room was showing off for Liz. They all saw her as a novelty, a prize, and even Jean's own children, in their youth, recognized the unspoken trophy of attention from a beautiful woman. It was a scene women like Jean, in all their dependable plainness, were forced to stand outside of many times over in their lives. She realized in that moment, many versions of this scene would be replayed for her over and over once Tommy and Liz were married.

Tommy had been mistaken. Liz was going to be fine.

On the counter next to her, lay a stray safety pin. Jean discreetly closed her fingers over it, then slipped her hand into her jacket pocket. There, she worked the pin open and, keeping her face passive and unchanged, holding her breath as she always did, pushed the tip of the pin into her palm. Burning pain seared through her flesh and up her arm like an electrical current, but she kept pushing, kept smiling at the playful banter before her, until the smile froze itself into a grimace. When she felt the wetness of blood on her fingertips, she extracted the pin and allowed herself to exhale.

She pressed a fingertip over the pin prick to stanch the bleeding and leaned against the wall behind her, the same wall that in the past had probably seen children and adults alike clamoring around pretty, happy Beatrice for the competition of her love and affection, while Eunice had been resigned to watch from a corner, on the outside of the circle.

Indeed, she and Eunice shared much more than a house.

CHAPTER 7

Labor Day, 1952

The Methodist Church Labor Day potluck was reminiscent of the Krenshaw's July Fourth picnic—food, families, and festivities like Jean had never before seen. For a town of barely two thousand people, Chickering felt like a booming community, blissfully unaware of its own smallness.

In the several Sundays Jean Gillman had attended services with the Krenshaws, she'd met many of the church members—half the town, it seemed—and they'd welcomed her as quickly and as warmly as the Krenshaws. Jean had never been so readily embraced as she was in Chickering, or as happy.

Jean rode to the church sandwiched between Jim and Tommy in the Krenshaw's pickup truck with a bowl of her potato salad balanced on her knees. She sat between the brothers quietly, content to just listen to them talk around her about the crops, chores, and their ailing grandmother. Beatrice had grown depressed since her sister's death. Jim was in the process of moving into his late Aunt Eunice's house and the brothers agreed it would be good for someone to live just across the driveway again to keep Beatrice company.

"You should really get a fancy bowl for your salad," Tommy said.

After a few seconds, Jean realized he was talking to her. She looked down at the plain plastic bowl in her hands. "Why?" she asked.

"Salad that good deserves a fancy bowl," Tommy said.

"Proper presentation. Someday I'll get you one." He was wearing the blue shirt she'd made him, just like he said he would.

Jean smiled.

"Was it your mother's recipe? For the salad?" Jim asked, keeping his eyes firmly on the road while he drove.

Jean turned to him, her reaction to his voice always like an afterthought. "What?" she said. "Oh, yes. My mother's recipe. Handed down from her mother."

Jim nodded seriously. "It's very good."

"Good?" Tommy cried. "It's goddamn amazing!"

Only Jean and Tommy laughed and she hugged the bowl tighter.

At the church, Jean, Tommy, and Jim entered the hot and crowded fellowship hall and Jean quickly began to sweat. She handed her salad and subpar bowl off to Mrs. Iverson, the reverend's wife, and the three took their place at the back of the long food line.

Tommy leaned over and whispered in Jean's ear. "I think Reverend Iverson did something to his hair recently."

The line moved forward and Jean took a few steps to close the gap behind Jim.

"What do you mean?" she whispered back. She studied the reverend's head where he stood greeting parishioners at the door.

"I think he started wearing a hairpiece earlier this summer," Tommy said.

"Really?"

"Yeah." Tommy nodded. "And it looks like a coonskin cap."

Jean stifled a laugh behind her hand.

Jim reached around her and poked his brother in the ribs with his finger. "Keep your voice down," he said. "You're embarrassing us."

But Jean didn't mind. She'd never been included on inside jokes like this before. It made her feel conspiratorial, but in a good way, like she'd been invited to join an exclusive club.

They finally reached a line of wobbly card tables of food and desserts. Bonnie stood amid the configuration of church ladies working in the kitchen.

"You're late," she said as soon as they reached her table of cold fruit salads.

"It's Jimmy's fault," Tommy said. "He drives like a slow-poke."

"You should take note," Bonnie said. "You drive too fast." She slapped a spoonful of pink marshmallow salad onto Tommy's plate so hard he nearly dropped it.

"Oh, Jean, I want to introduce you to the Dawsons," Bonnie said, pointing to a mother and daughter approaching the line.

Jean knew exactly who they were. She remembered Tommy's comments from the Fourth of July picnic and had been hoping to avoid them. She turned around to say something to Tommy, but he and Jim had suddenly and conveniently disappeared.

"Jean Gillman," Bonnie said, "this is Alma Dawson of Dawson's Drugstore and her daughter, Beverly. She graduated with Tommy."

"Nice to meet you, Jean," Alma said. She wore her thin hair in the same towering beehive from the picnic, only it was crooked today, as if one side had begun to melt in the heat and slide down the side of her head.

"Bonnie and Beatrice speak very highly of you," she said. Beverly was busy filling a second plate with deserts and paying not a lick of attention to Jean.

"Thank you," Jean said. She tried to sound gracious while searching for an excuse to escape.

"So, where's that Tommy?" Alma asked Bonnie. She stabbed her fork into a brownie on her daughter's plate and scraped off a large chunk. "Beverly is anxious to visit with him. They're such good friends, you know."

Beverly eyeballed the stolen piece of brownie as it moved from the plate to her mother's lips.

Jean noticed a middle-aged couple descending the stairs along with two young boys and a teenage girl. The girl scanned the crowd and smoothed down the front pleats of her knee-length skirt. Her white-blonde hair was nearly transparent beneath the fluorescent lights. Jean remembered her from the picnic as the pretty blonde she'd seen Tommy talking to.

Alma quickly set her plate down and leaned over the table toward Bonnie.

"Did I tell you what happened in the drugstore last week?" she said under her breath. "Rudy got into a nasty argument with old Milton Miller over a fence line between their properties." She continually glanced at the couple who had just entered and Jean deduced the story was about them.

Bonnie's eyes widened with interest. "Really?" she said. "That's terrible."

"Paulette was just mortified."

Bonnie nodded in silent agreement. "She should be."

Alma turned to Jean. "Sandy was one of the Alice in Dairyland finalists this year. She didn't win, though."

"A finalist," Jean said. "That's really something."

Alice in Dairyland was an annual, state-wide beauty competition that picked one girl from the "princess" finalists to be the agriculture ambassador of Wisconsin for twelve months. It was a highly coveted and competitive honor.

Alma continued. "Last spring I saw her giving away cheese cubes at Woodman's grocery in Janesville with the other princesses. She was by far the prettiest girl of the bunch. It's a shame she didn't win."

The family worked their way through the crowd and Jean began to make out the girl's round blue eyes and, closer still, a perfect scattering of pale freckles across the bridge of her nose.

"Hello, Rudy," Alma said.

"Hello, Alma," he said with a stern nod.

Alma wasted no time. "Sandy, I was just telling Jean that I saw you at Woodman's last spring when you were doing cheese as an Alice Princess. The Gorgonzola wasn't salty enough, but your dress was very smart."

"Oh, thank you," Sandy said.

"Beverly thought about trying out to be an Alice princess," Alma continued. "She's a natural at those things."

The group turned to look at Beverly, catching her in midbite of a second piece of brownie. She smiled weakly, her teeth dotted with bits of chocolate crumb.

"Oh, sure," Sandy said, fiddling with the top button on her blouse. Her wrist and fingers were long and delicate.

"So, who won this year?" Bonnie asked.

Sandy's mother, Paulette, laid her hand on her daughter's arm. "The girl from Independence," she said. "She was very poised."

"She was swell," Sandy added.

Jean watched Sandy's hands flutter about her body, skimming her hair and small features of her face as if to assure herself she was still in the flesh. Up close, Jean noticed a small chicken pox scar just above her left eyebrow.

"Did you get to hand out a lot of cheese?" Bonnie asked.

Sandy nodded. "I also greeted customers at the Fleet Wholesale Supply in Janesville one afternoon," she said.

"No, it was Blaine's Farm and Fleet in Janesville," Paulette said. "The new Mill's Fleet Wholesale Supply is in *Marshfield*."

"Oh, right!" Sandy said. "I always get them confused."

"And really, who cares," Bonnie said, dumping a glob of pink salad onto Paulette's plate.

Jean shifted from one aching foot to another as the conversation droned on around her. She spotted Tommy and Jim at a table in the corner and seized the opportunity to slip away from the group unnoticed. She stopped at the beverages to pour herself a glass of iced tea and inspected her swollen, ugly toes protruding from her sandals like raw sausages. Her feet always swelled in the heat when she stood too long. She wished she had worn her old canvas shoes to at least cover the unsightly swelling.

"Do you need help carrying anything?"

Jean looked up and found Sandy standing in front of her.

"No, thanks, I'm fine."

"Your name is Jean, right?"

"Yes."

"I'm Sandy. I remember you from the Krenshaw's picnic." She held out her hand and Jean gave it a quick shake.

"So where did you live before Chickering?" Sandy asked.

Jean hesitated before replying, not particularly interested in talking to the girl. "Helenville," she finally said.

"Oh," Sandy nodded. "That's a nice little town. Have you lived anywhere else?"

Jean shifted uncomfortably to her opposite foot and suppressed a sigh. "Um, well, let's see, before Helenville, we lived in Muscoda and Bell Center for a while, and before that Cold Spring very briefly, and before that I was born in Clermont, Iowa."

"My goodness! That's a lot of moving! I've lived in Chickering my whole life," Sandy said and flicked her hand with a peevish wave. "I've never been anywhere or seen anything. That's why I was trying for Alice in Dairyland. I wanted to travel and see new and interesting places."

"I don't know how interesting towns like Muscoda or Bell Center are," Jean said.

Sandy laughed. "Maybe you're right."

"But an Alice Princess, that must have been fun."

Sandy started to fidget and twist the top button on her blouse once more. "It was," she said. "I was really sorry I didn't win. Is it terrible to say that?"

Sandy's mannerisms and voice were nervous, restrained, not at all what Jean would've expected from an Alice Princess or someone so pretty, for that matter. Sandy reminded Jean of a crepe satin dress, the same light green color as her eyes, that Jean once helped her mother sew. The fine, silky fabric was beautiful, the most luxurious Jean had ever seen, but so fragile. The slippery material had easily snagged, the seams puckered, and even the slightest amount of heat from the iron left burn marks.

Sandy lowered her voice. "My father was against it at first." She glanced over her shoulder, as if checking for assurance he wasn't within earshot. "I had a hard time talking him into letting me do it. He's very strict." She twisted another button. "I don't know why I'm telling you all of this! I always talk too much around new people."

Jean finally offered a genuine smile. Crepe satin. Definitely. "I don't mind," she said and added without thinking, "My father's really strict, too."

"I should let you sit down and eat," Sandy said.

"Do you want to get some food?" Jean asked.

"No, I'm fine." She picked up Jean's glass of tea and a set of napkin-wrapped silverware as Jean gathered her plate of food, probably cold by now.

"I'm sitting over there," Jean said, gesturing to Tommy and Jim.

"Oh, sure." Sandy waved at the brothers and they waved back.

Jean sat down next to Tommy and Sandy pulled up an extra chair beside her.

"I see you two met," Tommy said.

"We did," Sandy said. She primly crossed her legs at the ankles and carefully arranged her skirt over her knees.

"Sandy and I were in school together," Tommy said to Jean.

"We've known each other since we were kids," Sandy

added. "I live just a few miles east of the Krenshaws. And a word of advice—Tommy Krenshaw is the biggest goof off you'll ever meet and the only reason he graduated is because he cheated off my math homework for four straight years."

"Hey!" Tommy dropped his fork and spread his arms in protest.

"I'm just kidding," Sandy said. She snatched up the fork and took a bite of chocolate pie from his plate.

Tommy silently slid the plate and remainder of the pie over to Sandy for her to finish it.

"I like your shirt," Sandy said. "Is it new?"

"Yep," Tommy said. "Jean, here, was nice enough to make it for me. And perfect timing, 'cause I tore the hell out of my gray shirt working on a barbed wires fence."

"It's really nice. You must be a good seamstress," Sandy said.

"I'm okay," Jean said, embarrassed by the attention.

Sandy blotted her upper lip with a napkin. "Gosh! I hate this weather!" she cried.

"Me, too," Jean said. She slipped off her sandals, revealing angry red strap marks across her puffy skin. "My feet always swell in the humidity." She shook her head in disgust.

Sandy's eyes widened. "Mine, too!" She kicked off her pristine, white canvas shoes. The tops of her bloated feet were also crisscrossed with red seam markings.

They held their feet out in front of them, displaying ten painfully inflated toes in a row, and laughed.

"It's like a parade of the world's ugliest feet!" Sandy said and they laughed again.

Tommy gathered the empty plates into a small pile. "I saw you talking to Alma and Beverly earlier. I split as soon as they showed up."

"They were practically interrogating Sandy," Jean said.

"My sympathies," Tommy said.

"Oh, you know Beverly and her mother are harmless,"

Sandy said.

Tommy grinned. "Remember in eighth grade when Alma showed up at school and yelled at Mrs. Fine for not giving Beverly the lead in the spring musical? What was the show?"

Sandy giggled. "*The Music Man.* Beverly was stuck in the chorus of singing townspeople with the rest of us. Where she belonged."

Tommy continued. "Or when Alma tried to hot roll Beverly's hair for the spring formal junior year and burned off a big piece in the back!"

"That wasn't funny, Tommy!" Sandy cried. "I actually felt sorry for her!" But despite her defense of Beverly, she continued giggling and trading stories with Tommy.

Jean folded her napkin in half and repeatedly smoothed the paper crease between her fingers, wearing it thin. This was how it always started in the small towns—some conversation about something funny involving someone she didn't know or some great event from the past that Jean had no idea about and couldn't share. She tried to keep a smile on her face as the conversation ping-ponged between Sandy and Tommy and even Jim at one point, but she couldn't help feeling as if her earlier membership to the exclusive club had suddenly been revoked.

Sandy stopped laughing and looked at Jean. "We're being rude, aren't we?" she asked. "What do you care about these dumb stories about people you don't even know?"

Jean shrugged. "It's okay."

"It's not. We were leaving you out." Sandy took the shredded napkin from Jean's hand and tossed it aside as if to prove her point. "We need to plan something fun for you to do this week while the weather is still nice. We should take you swimming at the lake."

Jean stiffened at the mere idea of a bathing suit and instinctively covered her arms with her hands, even though she was already wearing quarter-length sleeves. "Well," she said,

"I don't really know how to swim."

"Okay. I'll think of something else then." Sandy twirled her hair while she thought. "I've got it! Tommy, let's take her for a picnic next Sunday afternoon at Lake Koshkonong. We'll get a little group together and play some croquet. It'll be grand!"

And with that, Jean was back in the club, and for the first time in a new town, making a friend.

CHAPTER 8

December, 1963

Jean stood at her kitchen window washing the breakfast dishes, watching gray-smudged clouds build in the northwest with more snow. She rubbed the back of her neck, stiff from a poor night's sleep, while the children sat slack-mouthed on the living room floor, blissfully staring at the television. Cartoons were a treat only when their mother wanted them out of her hair and the annoyance of the television was more bearable than the annoyance of three boys roughhousing.

"Boys, don't sit so close to the screen or you'll ruin your eyes," she called.

She returned to the kitchen table where she was numbering plastic ear tags for the heifers with a permanent marker, and updating the cow records in a leather ledger.

It had been several weeks since the wedding—a quick, intimate ceremony at the Chickering Methodist Church with only close family members and friends present. Tommy had worn a smart brown suit and crisp white shirt while Liz had opted for a summery floral dress with a wreath of flowers in her hair, totally inappropriate for the chilly early winter weather.

Jean blew on a wet tag waiting for it to dry. Their wedding kiss had been deep and long. Tommy had pulled Liz tightly against his body and bent her back into a dip, while Liz had buried her fingers in his hair and opened her mouth wide. The glint of their tongues was visible even from the front row and Jean had never seen a wedding kiss like that before, like they were sharing a kiss in private, like no one else was in the room.

Jean looked down and realized that she'd smudged the ink on the tag with her finger. As she wiped the streak off with a rag, Larry wandered into the kitchen and began to hopscotch across the linoleum squares. Each time he landed, the old floor squeaked beneath his weight and the glass salt-and-pepper shakers rattled atop the stove.

"Why don't we bake your birthday cake today," Jean said. "What flavor do you want this year?"

"Yellow with chocolate frosting," Larry answered without hesitation. He stopped hopping and looked at her. "What did you want for your tenth birthday?"

Jean removed a large mixing bowl from the cabinet and measured out a cup of softened butter from a crock. "Let me think for a minute. It's been a long time since I was ten." She turned to replace the crock in the icebox and Larry met her movement by opening the door.

"Uncle T said that when he was ten he asked for a BB gun and got one, so I don't see why I can't get a pocketknife. Ten is a big deal. It's double digits."

Larry had been pestering anyone who would listen for weeks about a tortoise shell handle pocketknife he'd spotted at Blaine's Farm and Fleet.

"Okay, I remember what I asked for now," Jean said as she cracked an egg over the mixing bowl. "I wanted a set of paper cutout dolls like my neighbor, Becky Sue." Jean shook the last bit of sugar from the canister into a measuring cup. She opened a cabinet where her grocery list was tacked inside the door and bit the cap off a pen, holding it between her teeth as she added sugar to the neatly printed column.

"And did you get them?"

"Yes, I did. My mother ordered them from the Sears & Roebuck catalogue."

"See! Everyone gets what they want on their tenth birthday. It isn't fair."

"Paper dolls are hardly as dangerous as a pocket knife!" Jean clicked her tongue. "Your father just doesn't think you're responsible enough for a knife yet."

Larry flicked a crumb off the counter with his index finger. He narrowed his eyes at his mother, contemplating a response, and Jean had to stop for a moment to marvel at just how much the boy's expression, the same wrinkle between his brows when he frowned, resembled his uncle.

"Is this all a cover because you really bought me the knife?" Larry finally asked.

Jean shook her head and laughed.

Larry dunked his finger in the batter and licked it clean. "I bet Uncle T bought me the knife. Don't you think he probably bought me the knife?"

Jean shrugged. "I guess you'll just have to wait until the party to find out."

Larry slapped his hands on the counter, sending up a small cloud of flour. Jean poured the finished batter into two circular metal cake pans and Larry opened the oven door for her, and then let it spring back shut with a bang.

"I'm going out to get the mail," Jean said. "Are you coming with me?"

Outside, Larry clomped alongside Jean in a pair of Jim's old insulated boots, two sizes too big.

"Look," he continued. "If you know that someone got me the knife, you don't have to tell me. Just give me a little signal or something. Wink or itch the side of your nose. Then that way, if anyone asks if you told me, you technically won't be lying if you say no."

At the end of the driveway, Jean reached into the box to retrieve the mail. "I'm done talking about this, Larry," she said.

Larry crossed his arms over his chest and glowered. Jean

flipped through the stack and sorted the envelopes according to address. For as long as the twin houses existed, the residents had shared a mailbox. Recently, the Chickering Post Office had begun to pester the Krenshaws about switching to two separate boxes since they were implementing the new five-digit zip codes, but Jim and Tommy had refused. This was how it had always been done on the farm and they weren't about to be the ones to buck tradition. Jean had agreed. No need to reinvent the wheel.

She flipped through the envelopes, separating their mail from Tommy's, and now Liz's, but not before peeking at each and every return address. Nothing of interest, as usual.

"Go help your father clean stalls," she said, nudging Larry in the direction of the barn. "He could use the extra help."

"Fine." Before he turned to leave, he scratched the side of his nose. When Jean shook her head, Larry dropped his shoulders in defeat.

Jean followed the driveway to Tommy and Liz's house and couldn't help but smile to herself, knowing Tommy had bought the pocketknife several weeks ago when Larry first started talking about it. Even though she agreed with Jim that it was a dangerous gift for a ten-year-old, she could never bring herself to scold Tommy when he indulged her children.

On the porch, Jean peered through the frost-covered window of the storm door. She could see Liz sitting at the kitchen table alone, smoking a cigarette with a vacant stare. Since the wedding, Jean usually only saw her in the mornings when she dropped off their mail.

Jean rapped on the door and Liz roused from her seat to answer it. She greeted Jean wearing a tight appliquéd sweater and slim plaid pants that made her appear even more petite than usual, and bare feet. Jean marveled at the woman's apparently superior immune system. By comparison, she felt bulky and drab in her heavy wool coat and denim trousers.

"Hi," Liz said. She held the door open and Jean entered.

"Good morning," Jean said.

Liz didn't respond. Instead, she lit a cigarette without noticing another one was already smoldering in the palm leaf ashtray on the table. She slumped back into her chair. Her face was pale and she seemed tired, listless. The kitchen table was littered with schoolbooks and papers.

"Are you studying for a class?" Jean asked.

"Not anymore," Liz said. She tucked her feet beneath her and rubbed her bare toes. "I'm sort of taking a break from school. Tommy and I talked about it and we decided that it wouldn't be a good idea for me to drive back and forth to Madison during the winter."

Jean had never been interested in college, but once upon a time she had dreamed of opening a seamstress shop in Chickering. Little Chick Alterations, they were going to call it. She hadn't thought about the seamstress shop in a long time.

"I'm sure you'll get back in classes next spring," Jean said.

"Of course I will," Liz said, just short of snappish.

Jean uncomfortably looked away into the living room cluttered with opened boxes and tissue paper. "You're still opening wedding gifts, I see."

Liz shrugged. "We finished last night. We actually mailed out the last thank you note today." She lifted her thick hair up off her neck, momentarily exposing the intimate patch of soft skin and silky tendrils along her hairline.

Jean noticed that every time she asked Liz a question, the girl made a point to answer it as "we." She also knew about the notes, having received hers the previous day when it was personally couriered over by Tommy. She'd been surprised by Liz's decision to sign all the cards *Love, Liz and Tommy*, as opposed to the traditional, expected, *Sincerely, Mr. and Mrs. Thomas Krenshaw*. Not only had she scrapped the tactful Mr. and Mrs., but she also put her own name first, surely setting plenty of tongues wagging throughout the community as the wives of Chickering were greeted at their mailboxes by this ostentatious breach in etiquette.

"Speaking of mail," Jean said. "I brought yours." She held out the stack of envelopes to Liz. "I usually give it to Tommy when I bring over his lunch, but now that you're here," she paused, the words stuck in her throat. "I'll just give it to you."

Liz narrowed her eyes at the envelopes and blew a long, unattractive line of smoke through her nose. She lifted her stare from the envelopes, still suspended in Jean's outstretched hand between the two women, to Jean's face. Jean felt hot sweat suddenly break out beneath her arms and it sent her gaze darting uncomfortably about the room.

Liz finally accepted the small stack of mail and tossed it onto the table without another glance. "You know Jean," she said, crushing out the abandoned cigarette and tapping off the ash from the one in her hand. "There's something I think we should talk about—"

The screen door banged open and a cold breeze swept through the room.

"Ladies!" Tommy called, clapping snow off his work gloves. "Just in time to have some coffee with the two best Mrs. Krenshaws in the county!"

Jean smiled, but Liz took a drag from her cigarette. "I'll start a fresh pot," she said through an exhale of smoke.

"Thanks, Baby. Have a seat, Jean," Tommy kicked off his boots and dropped onto a chair.

Jean removed her coat and sat across the table from him. She nudged the scattered mail into a neat pile with her finger. Tommy's mere presence always made her feel a bit more relaxed around Liz.

"I've been dying to tell you something," Jean said. "The funniest thing happened at the bank yesterday with you-know-who's-what."

"Oh, Lord, here we go," Tommy laughed, shaking his head.

"This one is grand, I promise." She leaned forward and settled her elbows on the table. "I was at Judy Fresco's window when he walked in with his little grandson, Danny."

"The one with the lazy eye?"

"No, the other one."

"With the impetigo?"

"Right. That one. Anyway, he carried him into the bank and got in line behind me. He starts telling Judy about how Danny can count to one hundred even though he's only three and then tells Danny to do it for us all."

Tommy's smile grew wider as Jean talked. Liz removed sugar, cream and three mugs from the cabinet, occasionally turning her head as she listened, still unsmiling.

"He tries and tries to get Danny to do it but Danny keeps whining and hiding his face. Finally, Danny screams 'No!' and...and..." Jean paused, laughter already bubbling up before the finale. "He rips the thing off his granddaddy's head and throws it into a potted plant behind the teller's counter!"

Tommy threw his head back with a roaring laugh.

Jean also crumbled into a convulsive fit of laughter. "But then," she gasped, "Judy's back there, picking it out of the plant...brushing the dirt off..." She was laughing too hard to finish.

Tommy put his head down and beat his fist on the table. "Oh, my God!" he cried. "That's the best god damn one yet!"

Liz set her burning cigarette on the edge of the ashtray and crossed her arms over her chest. "He threw what into the potted plant? I don't get it."

Tommy stopped laughing and wiped his eyes. "Oh, his toupee. His hairpiece?"

"Whose hairpiece?"

Jean also stopped laughing.

"You know, Reverend Iverson," Tommy said. "I told you he wears one."

Liz shrugged. "I don't think you did." She turned back to

the percolating coffee.

Tommy shook his head, chuckling again. "That's funnier than the time he wore it crooked through an entire Easter service."

"Or when it got snagged on a tree branch at the church picnic," Jean said, excitedly pointing at him. "Do you remember that?"

"Oh, shit! Right! Mrs. Iverson needs to get that poor guy some hair glue or something. What's that stuff you used to glue the beard to my face when I dressed up as a hobo for the Legion Halloween party?"

"It was just a homemade paste I concocted. Flour and water and something else, I can't remember."

"Well, it smelled like ass."

Jean and Tommy started laughing again.

"Coffee!" Liz said, her voice slicing through the room.

Jean and Tommy fell instantly silent, the echo of their laughter hanging in the air.

"Coffee sounds great," Tommy finally said.

"Speaking of hobos," Liz said, handing Tommy a mug, "Do you remember the time we were leaving that diner in Madison and the homeless guy with the shopping cart started hassling you about your Cubs baseball cap?"

Tommy took a drink of the coffee and covered a laugh behind his hand. "Shit!" he coughed. "He kept yelling, 'It's the Milwaukee Braves, you dumb sonofabitch!'"

"And then he grabbed your hat and you chased him down the street until you got it back!" Liz added, also laughing.

"Oh, dear," Jean said, "that sounds like it was—"

"It's my lucky hat!" Tommy said. "I couldn't let him keep it."

"It sure is your lucky hat," Liz said with a coy smile, and Tommy leaned over and met her in the middle of the table with a deep kiss.

Jean jumped up and hastily gathered her coat. "I should

probably go."

Tommy pulled away from Liz. "You can't stay for one cup of coffee?" Tommy asked.

"No, I'm sorry," Jean said, fumbling to get her arms through the sleeves, her face hot. "Larry's birthday cake is in the oven."

"Next time, then," Liz said, and resumed smoking.

Tommy stood and opened the door for her. As she passed, he mussed the top of her hair with his hand. "Good ole Queen Jean," he said. "Just like I'd hoped. The Three Musketeers again."

Jean tried to smile for his benefit, but couldn't. She crossed the frozen yards and a cold gust of wind barreled up the driveway, sending a blinding swirl of icy snow into her face, stealing her breath and chilling her to the bone.

CHAPTER 9

September, 1952

After the church potluck, Jean discovered that she looked forward to visits with Sandy Weaver almost as much as visits with Tommy. Sandy made good on her word and took Jean to Lake Koshkonong for a picnic and croquet along with Tommy and Jim and a few other friends, and she continued to visit Jean regularly.

During the lingering hot days of a long Indian summer that cantankerously refused even one drop of rain for relief, Sandy helped Jean put up her garden. They stewed tomatoes split around the stem from the prolonged dry weather, canned bitter carrots, shriveled yellow-green beans, bell peppers, zucchini relish, and beets, the purple juice staining their fingertips like angry bruises. The wooden shelves of the fruit cellar already sagged under jars of strawberry jam, apple butter and pickled peaches, both spicy and sweet.

They chatted nonstop while they worked. Jean talked about her mother, about the different towns she'd lived in, all the moves she'd had to make and the loneliness she'd experienced. Sandy talked about her dreams of traveling, of getting out of Chickering, of her disappointment over losing Alice in Dairyland and all the opportunities that could've come with it. And they both talked about their difficult fathers.

Sandy, Jean decided, was the nicest person she'd ever met. She'd never had a best friend. The months since the Fourth of July picnic were the happiest she'd ever been and, for the first time in years, she didn't have a single cut or burn healing somewhere on her body.

Today they were canning the last of Jean's sweet corn. The ears were overripe and the dark yellow kernels were bloated and tough, but no food could go to waste, especially with lean winter months coming. They husked the remaining buckets of ears, blanching them one pot at a time in water boiled on the stove, and then moved them to a bowl of ice. They sliced off the kernels with the only two sharp kitchen knives in the house and filled Eunice's old mason jars, borrowed from Beatrice after Jean used up her own supply a week ago.

The pressure cooker whistled from the stove as the glass canisters inside clinked and rattled against each other. Sandy unfastened the clamps, opened the cooker lid, and stepped back to avoid the cloud of steam.

"I've been thinking," she said, extracting a jar with a pair of canning tongs. "We should save some of the best jars of the jam and apple butter and try to sell them at the church Christmas bazaar. We could cover the lids with pretty little scraps of material and tie ribbons around the necks. Make them look pretty. My mother has tons of extra material lying around the house. And there's the Chickering May Day celebration and the county fair and the Krenshaw's Fourth of July party. We could talk Tommy into helping us."

Jean slid a knife down the pimpled sides of an ear, juice popping and splattering her cheeks, mingling with the dotted layer of sweat across her forehead. "That's a good idea," she said. "And we could sell loaves of homemade bread with it."

"And biscuits," Sandy said. "And, oh my goodness, your potato salad! Everyone is so crazy about your potato salad! Think of the money we could make!" She became so excited she nearly dropped the hot jar.

"What would you do with the money?" Jean asked.

"Oh, gosh," she sighed. "If I could make enough money, I'd love to travel a little. I'd love to visit Chicago!"

"I've never been to Chicago," Jean said. "It's so big. I'd surely get lost."

"I think it would be so much fun to work in an office as a secretary."

Jean shook her head. "I'm a terrible typist."

Sandy fell silent for a moment. "Well, at any rate," she finally said, "I'll probably just end up marrying a farmer and staying in Chickering. Have a family."

"That's not so bad, is it?" Jean said.

Sandy set the last cooled jar in the ice bowl and dropped onto the chair next to Jean. "No," she said, "I guess not." She propped her chin in her hand and traced small circles on the table with her finger.

"When I was a little girl," Jean said, "I dreamed about having a seamstress shop where I could make dresses and blouses and skirts. I love to sew."

Sandy suddenly straightened and her eyes grew wide. "Jean Gillman, that's a brilliant idea!"

"What?"

She grabbed Jean's shoulders and gave her a shake. "A seamstress shop! In town! Think about it. All the ladies in Chickering have to drive to Janesville for major alterations or nice dresses. *We* could open a shop *here*. Together! You could do the sewing stuff and I could do the business stuff. We'd be a great team! We get along so well!"

Jean wrinkled her nose. "Us? Open a seamstress shop?"

"Sure! Why not? I mean, if I have to be stuck in Chickering, might as well be stuck here doing something fun. And for now we could sell as much of the canned and baked goods and your salad as possible to use as seed money for the shop."

"Would your parents approve?"

Sandy threw her hands in the air. "What would they have to object to? Come on, this is a great idea. We could look for some space on Main Street, like near the diner or something. Call it Little Chicks Alterations. Isn't that cute?"

Jean sat back against the chair and adjusted her glasses, thinking. It didn't take long before a full, detailed picture of a life began to emerge. A little seamstress shop in town with Sandy, her new best friend. If she continued to build a life in Chickering, maybe there would be marriage in her future. Her own home. Children. The kind of life she'd hardly dared allow herself to dream about before.

Slowly, a smile began to spread across her face.

"You like this idea, right?" Sandy said, seeing Jean's expression.

Jean nodded and Sandy smothered her face with a hug.

"This is so great!" Sandy cried.

Yes, Jean liked this idea very much.

Toad's truck rumbled down the driveway, the squeal of a loose fan belt preceding his arrival. Jean and Sandy jumped to their feet. Their elation from seconds earlier instantly evaporated. Sandy grabbed four jars in one deft motion and scurried down the stairs to the fruit cellar. She had learned quickly during their visits to always appear busy for Jean's sake whenever Toad was around. Jean went back to slicing an ear of corn.

The porch screen banged open, slamming into the wall behind it. Toad fixed his steely eyes on Jean and she held her breath, waiting, never able to predict his moods.

He stepped out of his boots and said, "I'm ready to eat."

She hurried to the icebox to fix him a sandwich.

Sandy returned from the cellar. "Hello, Mr. Gillman," she said.

Toad nodded at her.

"Jean, I'll see you tomorrow. We'll talk more about the idea later." She enthusiastically pumped her fists in the air behind Toad's back. Jean suppressed a smile and shooed her out the door. Her father wasn't the type of man who tolerated two daydreaming girls.

As soon as Sandy was gone, Toad emptied the contents

of his trouser pockets into a jumbled pile on the table. Jean handed him a ham sandwich on a plate. As he grabbed the sandwich, he accidentally knocked the plate out of Jean's hands. It fell to the floor and broke into several pieces.

"Sorry," Toad mumbled and rubbed his face, leaving a smear of grease across the side of his nose from his grimy fingers. He grabbed a bruised, yellow apple out of the bowl on the table and went back outside, taking his sandwich with him.

Jean sighed and stooped down to clean up the broken pieces. Her thoughts immediately returned to Sandy's proposal. *Little Chicks Alterations.* Her stomach flipped with excitement. There would be so much to do, so much to plan, but the more she thought about it, the more she agreed with Sandy, it was a great idea. It could possibly work. Her own money could finally mean freedom.

She started a mental walking tour of Main Street, scrutinizing the storefronts that made up what constituted the downtown. Her mind finally landed on the small building that Sandy was talking about, a building that had been vacant since Jean's arrival. It was the perfect size with a nice picture window and was ideally situated between the Little Chick Diner and the beauty salon, and was directly across the street from the post office. The women of Chickering passed it regularly. Jean could already see the name Little Chicks Alterations painted in neat, bright letters on the glass window.

She stood with the dustpan in her hand and glanced around for a piece of paper, thinking to jot a few of these ideas down before she forgot them. Her eyes skimmed over the discarded items from her father's pocket scattered on the table: loose change, a dirty handkerchief, a ring of keys, a handful of peanuts, and a dark blue pocket book. His Chickering Savings and Loan bankbook, she realized, which he normally kept hidden in his bedroom.

She lifted the cover and expected to see her father's haphazard writing in the columns on the first page. It was blank. She sat down hard on the chair and flipped through the rest of the pages. Also blank. Her mind reeled. There had not been a single deposit since they had moved to the hog farm. Not a single payment to the bank.

Jean dropped the dustpan, spilling the broken pieces of the plate.

She glanced out the window to ensure her father was nowhere in sight, and began a search. She started with his usual hiding places for papers and other things he considered none of her business—the pockets of his coat hanging in the mudroom, loose floorboards in the kitchen, the tops of cabinets—but found nothing. She moved down the hall to his bedroom where she rifled through the pockets of all his trousers that were mostly full of holes, the drawers of his bureau, the single drawer of his rickety nightstand that held only a Bible, and finally the top shelf of his closet, which was bare. As she was about to give up, she lifted the saggy mattress on his bed, and there she found an envelope from the Chickering Savings & Loan with a bright red stamp on the front marked NOTICE. She had found letters like this before, at their old farms in Helenville and Muscoda. She didn't have to open it to know what it said.

Toad Gillman had already defaulted on the farm rent. Once again, they would be evicted. Once again, they would have to move.

The detailed picture that had formed so vividly and hopefully in her mind just moments ago already felt like another lifetime.

She dropped the mattress onto the springs with a thud, kicking up a small cloud of dust motes. She walked back downstairs on what felt like wooden legs and went about cleaning up the kitchen, filling the sink basin with water to wash the dirty utensils, wiping down the counter, lining up the finished jars ready to shelve in the cellar.

There had been signs in recent weeks. She'd just refused to see them because she was so happy here. There was the visit to the farm from a man in a suit—someone from the bank, she now assumed—that Toad refused to discuss. Twice, she discovered her can of grocery money empty. And three days ago she'd noticed the unexplained disappearance of a valuable mantle clock that had belonged to her grandparents. That type of mysterious "disappearance" occurred at the other farms as well, with other items of moderate value, and even though she never asked her father about them, she knew who was taking the items and why. It happened enough over the years that Jean learned to carefully hide her most prized and valuable possession: her mother's genuine pearl necklace. That, she smartly kept hidden in its black velvet box behind the jars of beets in the fruit cellar. She'd caught Toad searching her bedroom before, and she knew exactly what he'd been looking for.

She lifted the bowl of ice water to dump it in the sink but paused. They would have to move again. The thought settled around her shoulders like a heavy yoke.

Jean set the bowl back down and plunged her hands below the surface of the ice cubes. She closed her eyes and forced herself to hold her hands still, even as her skin began to burn, her fingers ache, her muscles scream. She kept holding them down as minutes ticked by, as her arms trembled, her breath quavered, and tears ran down her cheeks.

CHAPTER 10

July 4, 1964

Jean read the recipe card aloud and added each item to the oversized bowl accordingly: eggs, sugar, milk, heavy cream, vanilla and salt, the latter poured in by James. Once mixed with a bag of crushed ice, Jean dumped the contents into the freezer bucket of her new electric ice cream maker, purchased from the Montgomery Ward catalogue. She plugged in the cord, allowing James the honor of flipping the switch, and the machine ground to life. They stood nearly shoulder-to-shoulder in the kitchen, James standing on a chair, and hypnotically watched the top stem of the dasher turn in slow, tight circles.

After several minutes, she removed the lid and James dipped a spoon inside for a taste.

"You need to put in more salt," he said. "It's too runny."

Jean shook her head. "It doesn't need more salt."

"I think it does."

"It just needs to mix a little longer."

"The directions say to add more salt." James thrust the printed pages into his mother's face.

Jean sighed and removed her glasses to clean a smudge from the lens on the corner of her blouse, then glanced at the instructions. "It needs more salt," she mumbled.

"Told you so," James said. He held up the Morton's box and shook it. "It's empty."

"I think I've got some more around here somewhere."

She rummaged through the kitchen cabinets but came up empty-handed.

It was the morning of July Fourth, and another party. Jean had purchased the ice cream maker in hopes of capturing a small piece of last year's enthusiasm, but an ice cream maker was hardly competition with a state-of-the-art milking machine and an engagement, and it was turning out to be more work than it was worth.

She dropped onto a chair next to James and winced at a cut she'd inflicted on the back of her leg where the generous flesh of her buttocks met her thigh. She rested her elbows on her knees and cupped her chin in her hands, her old childhood pose when she would sit on the back porch of the Clermont house and watch her mother hang wet laundry on the clothesline. She thought of what she might have been doing one year ago, at this exact time. Frosting brownies, she remembered. Mixing her potato salad in the crystal bowl she no longer possessed, but still acutely missed. Hardly a care in the world, just a year ago. It was inconceivable that a mere twelve months had passed since first meeting Liz.

"Mama," James said, stirring the runny concoction with a wooden spoon. "It's starting to melt."

Jean sighed and heaved herself to her feet. "I'll go over to Uncle Tommy's house and see if he has any salt we can use."

She slipped on her canvas shoes and walked out the door.

Each time she crossed the yards now, she was forced to pass by Liz's garden. For a full week that spring, Jean had watched from her kitchen window as Liz dug up and hoed a patch of earth at the edge of the yard, measured out rows, patted down seeds into the overturned earth, and stuck Popsicle sticks into the ground to label each section: rosemary, sage, onion, basil, and lavender. In the far north corner, a lone watermelon vine had started to flourish with one perfectly fat, oblong green melon. Late one night, unable to stand her curiosity any longer, Jean crept over and weighed the watermelon with a grain scale. Eight pounds before the first of July.

What really drove Jean crazy, though, was that once the garden had been planted, Liz did nothing more to care for it. She never watered it. She never weeded it. She never sprayed for bugs. And yet, every one of the seeds Liz put in the ground sprouted to full, lush plants amid the Foxtail and Morning Glory weeds, not to mention that damned watermelon. Each time Jean lugged the hose over to her own garden, or spent backbreaking hours pulling silkweeds out of her carrots and radishes, or spraying the armies of melon bugs devouring *her* watermelon vines, she couldn't help but look across the drive at the modest plot and feel hot waves of irritation ripple down her spine.

Jean climbed the steps of the porch and forced herself not to look at the garden. She rapped hard on the screen and Liz yelped from the kitchen.

"Sorry," Jean said. "I didn't mean to startle you."

"No, no, it's fine," Liz said. She dried her hands on a towel and held the door open for Jean to enter. She had pin-curled her hair, and was weaing a colorful floral sundress that complimented her dark skin.

"I don't mean to bother you," Jean said, "but I was wondering if you had a box of Morton salt I could borrow? I ran out and I'm in the middle of mixing homemade ice cream."

Liz beckoned Jean into the kitchen. "Let me take a look. I think I've got some." She checked the cabinet above the stove and produced a box. "Yep. Right here."

She handed it to Jean.

"Thank you," Jean said, and reached for the door handle to leave.

"I actually need to borrow something, too," Liz said. "A large bowl. For a salad I made."

Jean let go of the door. "What kind of salad?"

Liz hesitated. "Potato salad. Tommy said you usually run

out every year, so I thought I'd make some too, just so we have enough. I got this great recipe from a magazine."

Jean felt the muscles in her face grow tense. She nodded. "How thoughtful of you."

Liz waved her hand. "It was no trouble. But I don't have anything nice that's big enough and Tommy said he thought you had a crystal bowl that I could use."

Jean stiffened. "I...I don't have that bowl anymore," she said. "It got broken last summer."

"Oh. That's too bad."

"I might have a Tupperware bowl that's big enough, though."

"Great."

"I'll have James bring it over."

"Thank you."

The women stared silently at each other for an awkward moment before Jean finally turned to leave. Liz followed her onto the porch. Outside, the pleasant morning air had burned off and turned muggy.

"Your potted herbs look nice," Jean said, gesturing to the little terra cotta pots arranged in a neat row along the railing.

"I potted them from clippings from my garden for anyone who wants them," Liz said. "Mostly rosemary and sage."

A pesky fly began to nick at the corners of Jean's eye. She swatted it away and slowly moved down the steps, one at a time.

She purposefully avoided looking at the garden again. "That was nice of you," she said. "The ladies will enjoy them, no doubt."

Liz stood on the top step and crossed her arms over her chest. "I was telling Alma Dawson about my watermelon the other day. She says I should enter it in the county fair next week. Wouldn't that be a hoot if I won something?"

Jean forced a tight smile. "Oh, sure. You should do that."

"Well, I'll see you later then." Liz waved and disappeared

inside the house.

Jean rubbed her forehead with her fingers, still sticky from the ice cream. In a few hours the driveway and yard would fill with cars and trucks and bodies and incessant chatter about the weather and the crops, and she would have to stand next to Liz and their dueling bowls of salads and smile and nod at it all. She looked over the croquet course she had designed and set up, the hayrack wagon she had filled with fresh hay. She looked over the red, white, and blue checkered tablecloths she had sewn, and felt a flash of anger so intense she could've set the barn on fire if she'd been standing next to it.

She started walking again. The box of salt felt heavy in her hands. In the distance, out of the corner of her eye, she could see the green rind of Liz's fat watermelon shining in the sun as if it had been polished with furniture wax.

She willed her legs to deliver her back to her own house, but they seemed to have minds of their own, and instead carried her straight to the old chicken coop. There, she set the box down on the ground and flung open the rickety wood door. She rummaged around the piles of junk, empty boxes, and gardening tools looking for what, she wasn't exactly sure, until she spotted a small container of antifreeze sitting on the windowsill.

Metal can in hand, she calmly walked around the backside of the shed to the far corner of Liz's garden where, with no one in sight, she slowly poured every last drop of the antifreeze over the watermelon vine. When she was finished, she returned the empty can to the shed, picked up the salt and walked back to her house, feeling much better.

CHAPTER 11

October, 1952

Jean often thought about the things she was forced to leave behind each time she and her father moved and there was no room left in the back of the pickup truck: a porch swing she'd loved to lounge on as a child during warm summer nights, an old steamer trunk that had been handy for storing winter blankets, extra pots and pans, extra mason jars, piles of scrap material stored in old fruit crates she'd hoped to use on a new quilt, a fine set of leather-bound encyclopedias (mysteriously missing "A" and "F"), boxes of Christmas decorations, boxes of letters and papers, and a beautiful cherry wood bedroom vanity.

And she often thought about the valuable items in their home that went "missing" over the years: a sterling silver tea set her mother had received as a wedding gift, a Tiffany lamp, a working Corona typewriter that had belonged to her grand-father, the beautiful white and gold cradle Jean had slept in as an infant, and most recently, the mantle clock.

Prior to the rough year in Helenville, Toad and Jean lived on a farm outside of Muscoda, a few miles from the Wisconsin River on yet another rented farm. There, they raised not only hogs but also chickens, and it was debatable which had smelled worse. They lasted barely a year when Toad got into a squabble over unpaid rent with the owner. Before Muscoda, it was Bell Center—Jean's least favorite farmhouse with only a wood stove for heat, drafty windows, and no indoor plumbing. They stuck it out on that farm for over three years and the only things Jean missed about it when they left were the apple and pear orchards next to the house and an elderly female neighbor, crippled with arthritis, who would give Jean a dozen free eggs every week in exchange for mending and light housework. At least they never went hungry in Bell Center, unlike the six months in Cold Spring when her mother was dying.

The house Jean most fondly remembered was the sweet little two-story near Clermont, Iowa, where she spent much of her childhood. The Clermont house was her mother's house and it had always smelled of warm things—pies out of the oven, pot roast and potatoes, crackling fires in the hearth. Marjorie had painted the outside a cheerful yellow color and planted lilac shrubs around the porch, providing an ideal place to hide, daydream and stay cool during long summer afternoons. The land was flat and fertile and it was the only farm Jean could remember her father happy.

But once her mother became sick, the medical bills overwhelmed Toad and he lost the house and property to bankruptcy and they were forced to move to the farm outside Cold Spring, where Marjorie died shortly thereafter. His bitter anger mounted quickly and spilled over onto Jean, who was too weak to work a farm, but still too young to marry off for someone else to deal with.

From her sickbed in the final months before her death, Margie Gillman sensed Jean's precarious situation. She'd started teaching Jean how to sew her own clothes and curtains, how to darn threadbare socks, replace split zippers, and bake bread from scratch, sometimes shouting the directions from her sickbed in another room. Her voice, even in its weakened state, sounded hurried, urgent.

"Use your shoulders when you knead dough, Marjorie Ann. Now punch it with your fists!"

Margie knew she was dying and that her daughter would

be left alone with Hank, still known by his Christian name in those days, and she was frightened for what would become of Jean, motherless at such a young age.

"Just remember that your father's bark is worse than his bite," Margie repeatedly said. She would then add in a hushed, persistent voice, "And remember, always remember, God helps those who help themselves."

Jean was thinking of all this as she sat at the kitchen table, distractedly cutting a tough piece of ham into slices.

God helps those who help themselves.

She wasn't sure she believed this anymore.

It had been days since her last visit with Sandy and the grand plan for the seamstress shop. Jean had been avoiding her, making excuses on the telephone because she couldn't bear to see her friend in person yet.

The blade slid off the meat and sliced the outside edge of her index finger. She gasped and clutched the bleeding finger in her free hand, tears of pain spilling from her eyes. She rushed down the hall to the bathroom, leaving a dotted trail of blood behind her. There, she turned on the faucet and stuck her finger in the cloudy, lukewarm well water. Dizzy from the pain, she sat on the cracked toilet lid next to the sink and rested her forehead against the side of the basin. When she purposely hurt herself, the pain was always expected, desired, even. But, when an accident, she wasn't prepared and it was a shock.

Jean lifted her head to look at the finger and found a deep gash spreading from the first knuckle joint to the nail, like the hinged mouth of a snapdragon flower when squeezed. It probably needed stitches.

She dried her hand and found a gauze bandage in the medicine chest. She awkwardly bit off strips of medical tape with her teeth and scolded herself for being so careless, lost in her own self-pity and not paying attention.

The hard clomp of her father's boots crossed the wooden

porch steps followed by the squeak and slap of the screen door. Jean quietly closed the bathroom door and locked it. She waited. After a moment, Toad mumbled to himself and began slamming kitchen cabinet doors. The silverware drawer crashed to the ground. Toad cursed and continued talking to himself. He'd been drinking, Jean could tell. The sound of more doors opening and closing, items being tossed to the floor.

The door to the fruit cellar creaked open and Toad's boots thundered down the wooden stairs. Jean put her hands over her mouth and held her breath, but within seconds she heard the unmistakable sound of jars shattering against the ground, one after another, after another.

"Stop! Stop!" she cried, and fumbled with the lock on the door before finally jerking it open. She ran down the hall, tripping over her own clumsy feet and falling onto her cut hand. She quickly regained her footing but by the time she reached the kitchen, Toad stood at the top of the stairs with the black velvet necklace box in his hands.

Toad's watery eyes were bloodshot and dark moons of perspiration had formed under his arms and around the collar of his cotton shirt. Jean stared at him as her entire body shook, her chest heaving with short gasps. Her skin had gone cold.

"You been hiding this from me?" He held the box up and moved toward her. She recoiled.

"Answer me!" he shouted. "We're nearly starvin' to death and you're hiding *jewelry* from me?"

"They were my mother's—" she started to say but he raised his fist and charged at her. She backed away, bumping into the table. She put her hand down for support. Terror seized her by the throat. He'd never struck her before. Her fingers found the smooth wooden handle of the butcher knife, abandoned next to the slices of ham. In one swift reflex, as fast as her own shallow breath, she brought the knife up at arm's length with dead aim at Toad's heart. He froze, his forward momentum halted as if he'd hit an invisible wall. She'd seen hibernating honeybees do this very thing in winter when they'd charged out of a disturbed honeycomb, mad as hell, only to hit the sub-zero air and drop like rocks.

The shiny tip of the blade wavered in her shaking hand. They stayed like this for several seconds, father and daughter, each unmoving. Finally, the tight lines around Toad's mouth loosened.

"You shouldn't have hid these from me," he said. And with the velvet box still in his hand, he backed away. He removed his hat from a nail by the door, placed it on his head, and left.

Jean waited until all that was left was the curling dust trail of Toad's truck before she dropped the knife, sagged to the floor, and began to cry.

After some time, a soft voice called to her from the door.

"Jean?" Tommy pushed the screen open. "Are you okay?"

She removed her glasses and wiped the tears from her face.

He entered the kitchen and sat down next to her. "I heard," he said. "I was on the porch."

"The pearls. They were my mother's..." she started to say, but couldn't finish the words.

"I'm sorry," Tommy said. "Maybe he'll bring them back?"

She shook her head. "He won't bring them back," she said bitterly. "They're gone." She covered her face with her hands.

"I don't know why he hates me so much," she cried.

"Oh, now, he don't hate you," Tommy said, scooting closer and wrapping an arm around her shoulder. "He's just a tough old son of a bitch. He don't know any other way to be."

He pulled her tighter to him. "What happened to your hand?"

Jean looked down and saw that a red bloom had formed through the hasty bandage and several strips of tape were peeling loose.

"I accidentally cut it."

"Let me have a look." Tommy took her by the elbow and helped her into a chair. He held her injured hand in his own and carefully removed the tape and gauze.

"It's deep," he said. "You need a doctor."

Jean shook her head. "I can't pay for a doctor."

"Got any more of that tape?"

"Medicine chest in the bathroom," Jean said.

Tommy retrieved the roll of tape and the gauze and a bottle of peroxide from the bathroom. He sat on a chair facing her.

"Now, this'll hurt, but you gotta make sure it's clean." He uncapped the bottle and took her hand once more, holding it between his knees. He splashed the peroxide over her finger and she took in a sharp breath, clenching her eyes shut as white bubbles erupted on the wound.

"It stings!" she cried, curling her bare toes into tight balls.

"Here." He grabbed a bottle of Toad's whiskey from the liquor cabinet. "Drink this." He clumsily unscrewed the cap and dropped it, trying to juggle both her hand and the flask. Jean watched the cap roll across the floor in a large arc before it disappeared underneath the stove.

She hesitated, having never tasted liquor before, but then tipped the bottle to her lips and took a mouthful. The warm liquid burned a path from the back of her throat to the pit of her stomach, and she took comfort in the pain. She coughed and sputtered, thinking for a moment she might vomit before her roiling belly settled.

Tommy stuck three pieces of the white medical tape to the edge of the table and arranged the gauze on her finger. His hands trembled while he worked.

"I sure hate seeing a lady in pain," he said.

Jean took another drink. "It feels a little better."

"That's the whiskey talking."

She laughed out loud and suddenly became very aware of her hand pressed between his knees.

"I'm gonna do this butterfly tape my Grammy shown me."

"Okay." Jean felt a warm current spreading from where his fingers cradled her wrist to where his thumb pressed against the heart of her palm. He bent toward her in concentration while applying the crosswise pieces of tape. He was so close she could hear his steady breathing.

"I think my father is going to lose the farm," she whispered. "We'll have to move again."

He looked up from her hand and into her eyes. "Are you sure?"

She nodded.

"Aw, Jean. I'm sorry." He patted her bare knee.

"I really like it here," she said. "Sandy, and Beatrice, and Jim. You."

He smiled and cocked his head to the side. "I've never seen you without your glasses before," he said. "You look, pretty."

Jean blushed furiously. Tommy went back to work. He wound a piece of tape around her finger and she stared at the top of his head, at his thick waves of hair. She plucked out a piece of straw hidden in the locks and smoothed the disturbed hairs back down with a slow, gentle stroke of her free hand, finding his temple and his cheek. Tommy straightened.

She realized then that in the picture she'd formed with Sandy and the seamstress shop, Tommy had been a part of it. Her own home. Possibly marriage and children. Possibly becoming a Krenshaw. Part of a loving, respected family. Life on their successful farm. The July Fourth picnic every year.

Jean leaned toward him, balancing on the edge of the chair, until her lips met his. Every muscle in her body felt as if it were tightened into perfect alignment, like the wires in a finely tuned piano. His lips were as soft and warm as she'd imagined they would be.

Tommy pulled away and put his hand on her shoulder. "Jean," he said, dropping his head. "I'm sorry."

She turned her face away from him. The swell of her humiliation filled the room.

"I should go," he said, and stood.

She clenched her eyes shut for a moment and buried her hands in her lap.

He pushed his chair under the table and straightened his hat. "Be sure to change that bandage a few times a day."

Jean nodded. "Okay."

Tommy cleared his throat. He stopped at the door. "You still coming to church with us tomorrow?"

She forced a smile.

"Sure. Of course," she said, and pressed her nails through the gauze into the cut on her finger, digging, gouging, as hard as she could.

Still smiling, as though nothing—absolutely nothing—had happened.

CHAPTER 12

October, 1952

The next morning, Jean sat on her porch in her Sunday dress, waiting for the Krenshaw's old Chevy pick-up. A satisfying autumn breeze murmured through the pines on the west side of the house. She shielded her eyes against the bright easterly sun as the silver truck turned into the drive and lurched to a stop. From the bleached cloud of dust, Jim emerged.

"Mornin'," he said.

"Good morning." Jean adjusted the hem of her dress, tugging it over her bony knees. "Where's Tommy?"

"He offered to stay behind and deliver a calf."

Jean's hand fell from her eyes. "Oh."

A morning haze had settled over the hay field just beyond the yard, and she could hear the faint chirp of a bobwhite bird in the pines.

Jim sat down on the steps next to her. "What happened to your hand?" he asked.

She pressed the bandaged finger into her lap. "I cut it. It's nothing. I'm terribly clumsy. Always accidentally nicking or burning myself in the kitchen." Her first lie of many to him about the injuries.

He tugged at the tight collar of his shirt, which looked like it was nearly choking him. "You're probably disappointed Tommy didn't come."

"No," Jean answered quickly, turning to him. "Why would you think that?"

"I don't know. He's a lot more fun to be around than me."

"No, not at all," she said.

Jim removed his seed corn cap. "Jean, I know I ain't much to look at and I'm not so good with the girls and all," he said. "Not like my brother or anything, but I like you." His fingers walked back and forth along the bill of the hat. "There's a fall festival in Janesville next Friday night. I was thinking that maybe me and you could go."

Jean turned and stared incredulously at Jim, at his stiff and uncomfortable posture, as her brain tried to catch up to what he was saying. It was as if she'd just been informed that grass was purple, and all along she'd been walking on grass believing it to be green, but was now seeing it accurately, for the first time, as purple. In all the time she'd known Jim, she'd regarded him merely as Tommy's brother, a casual friend, an afterthought.

"I've been wanting to ask you out since the picnic," Jim said. "And last night Tommy told me about your father's troubles with the farm. That you might be moving."

Jean winced. "He told you about that?"

"Don't be sore with him. He knew I was kind of sweet on you. He was just trying to help."

Jean listened intently as she studied the spidery red lines in his cheeks, his long lashes, pale gray eyes. She looked down at his hands, remembering their calloused feel, and tried to imagine them caressing her cheek. Jim Krenshaw was sweet on her, she repeated.

Jean closed her eyes and tipped her face toward the sun.

And remember, always remember, God helps those who help themselves.

Jean opened her eyes and took his nervous fingers, still skittering along the bill of the hat, and gathered them into her own.

"Yes," she finally said. "I would like to go to the festival with you on Friday."

Jim raised his brows in surprise, as if he'd fully been expecting a rejection. "Yeah? Okay, then."

The breeze rustled again. The bobwhite bird chirped once more.

She would go to church with him and sit with the Krenshaw family. And maybe there would be more Sundays to come, and a life in Chickering after all. The little seamstress shop in town with Sandy. And maybe she would still become a Krenshaw. Part of a loving, respected family. Life on their successful farm. The July Fourth picnic every year. The same picture, but with slightly different colors.

Jean held Jim's hand and stroked the rough skin of his palm with her index finger. They sat in silence.

You cut your coat according to your cloth, her mother used to say.

CHAPTER 13

July, 1964

A few days after the party, Liz's watermelon vine shriveled up and died.

It was the best Jean had felt in months.

Emboldened, she tried antifreeze again, this time on the rosemary plants. The rosemary also died within a few days, and it gave Jean deep satisfaction to finally see Liz out in the garden on her hands and knees desperately pulling weeds or lugging buckets of water from the spigot like they were stop-loss measures. So deep was the satisfaction, in fact, that Jean hadn't cut herself in weeks.

She continued the antifreeze treatment. She sneaked out just after dinnertime or sometimes in the early morning, and swiftly emptied the container under the cover of darkness. She dumped it on the basil, the oregano and the mint. She worked out a system where she would pour it into the ground around the base of the plants and let it soak deep into the soil, and then finished them off with a light watering over the plants themselves. The treatments felt mischievous but not devious until she accidentally left the container out all night with the lid off and a raccoon licked it clean and died. She felt terrible and buried the raccoon between the two silos, vowing to be more careful.

Early one morning, antifreeze container in hand, planning to douse some tomato plants, she rounded the corner of the chicken coop and was startled to find herself face-to-face with a cow. In fact, several cattle were milling about the yard, munching geraniums and stepping on her pumpkin patch. Jean stepped away from the coop to see more cows pushing their way through the unlatched gate of the heifer lot behind the house. She dropped the container and ran toward the stanchion barn.

"Tommy!" Jean yelled. "Tommy! Heifers are out!"

The milk house door swung open and Tommy appeared, wiping his hands on a paper towel, still wearing his rubber apron.

"What?" he answered, unconcerned until he saw the escaped animals, and then he broke into a sprint. At the commotion, Jim emerged from the hay barn where he'd been feeding cattle and immediately scrambled to close the gate of the heifer lot.

Jean grabbed two leather whips from the machine shed and handed one to Tommy. They snapped the whips at a particularly unruly cow making a run for the road. Young and not yet bred or milked, heifers could be the most tempestuous members of the herd.

"Jean! There!" Jim pointed to the south field and slapped the rear of a cow to get her back onto the lot. "Two heading for the bunker!"

In late July, Tommy and Jim had erected a bunker silo to accommodate more silage for the growing herd. It was a twenty-foot tall concrete structure resembling a rectangular above-ground swimming pool but open on one end to access the feed throughout the year. Currently empty and awaiting the harvest, it was apparently an irresistible playground for two rogue heifers.

Jean jogged the rocky lane that cut behind the house and calf huts, to the turned ground of the hay field where the bunker now stood. Flimsy leather sandals were all wrong for running on sharp gravel, and her feet began to hurt. The heifers clopped up the small incline of the open bunker end and triumphantly trotted a path around the interior perimeter. Jean finally reached the bunker, too breathless to yell any commands, and brandished her whip to at least keep them corralled in a far corner.

The old Dodge half ton and cattle trailer careened down the gravel drive, gears grinding and brakes squealing. Jean barely had time to step aside as Tommy maneuvered the truck and trailer into a blockade position across the open end, and emerged from the cab clutching a cattle prod.

"Need some help?" he said.

"Yes," Jean panted, bent over at the waist with her hands on her knees.

He opened the trailer gate and released the ramp. "Stay at this end. I'll run 'em up from behind." He pointed directions with the electric prod and Jean moved closer to the trailer.

Tommy strode to the far end where the heifers paced with a nervous skitter. He made a wide circle, pinning them together in one corner, and then expertly ran them straight up the middle to where Jean waited, directing them to the ramp with whistles and the whip. As the last cow fought her way inside the trailer, she swatted Jean in the face with her tail, sending Jean's glasses flying to the ground. She slammed the gate shut once the cows were safely inside and secured the lock.

"Have mercy!" Tommy said. "Nice way to start the day."

Jean sagged against the side of the truck and mopped her forehead with a tissue from her breast pocket. She removed one of her sandals to pick out a pebble embedded in the thick skin of her heel. Tommy bent down and retrieved her glasses, inspecting one of the cracked lenses.

"Aw, heck," Jean said, taking them from him. "I've barely had these a year."

"That's the pits," Tommy said. A peculiar expression crossed his face then.

"What?" she asked.

"Nothing."

"What? Tell me."

"It's just...It's been a long time since I seen you without your glasses."

They held each other's gaze until Tommy looked away and Jean quickly slipped the glasses back on.

Jean noticed he was wearing a light blue button up shirt, and she nearly did a double take. It was almost identical to the blue shirt she'd sewn for him years ago. The top two buttons at the collar were left undone, exposing his pronounced collarbone.

Jean thought of the first spring she and Jim were married, when Tommy had taught her to drive. He would take her out in the old Dodge to one of the fallow hayfields, usually while Jim was working on some pressing task that ranked above all else. Tommy would gently talk her through working the clutch and gearshift as she drove jerky circles around the perimeter of the field. They laughed whenever she killed the engine or cut too close to the timber edge, long oak branches scraping the windows. And she remembered one particular Sunday afternoon, just home from church, when he'd taken her for a driving lesson wearing the blue shirt she'd made for him, unbuttoned at the collar, the way his shirt was now. And she clearly remembered glimpsing that small dip of smooth skin at the center of his collarbone, like a shallow pool, and wondering what it would smell like if she pressed her nose to it.

The agitated cows rustled inside the cramped trailer, nudging and kicking at the walls. Jean tossed her whip into the truck bed. She took note of one particularly large crack on an east wall panel and thought to point it out to Jim if she remembered. He was endlessly repairing the splintery fractures with tar.

Tommy sighed and played with the cattle prod, zapping the edge of his boots. "I suppose it's going to be a blistering one again today."

"I think so." Jean nodded and looked up at the clear sky. "Liz'll be cranky."

"Why is that?"

"The heat gives her headaches. Makes her more tired."

Tommy was smiling to himself, staring at the hayfield in front of them, the corners of his mouth turned up. He looked like the cat who ate the canary, as her mother used to say. She was about to ask why he was smiling, when he spoke.

"You think she's doing okay out here?" he asked. "Living on the farm?"

"Sure," Jean said and shrugged. "She's doing great. She seems like she's...adjusted." She removed her other sandal and brushed the dirt from the bottom of her foot and thought about Liz's garden and her strategic salad during the Fourth of July. Yes, she wanted to assure him, Liz had adjusted fine.

Tommy wrapped his arm around Jean and pulled her against his side. "You've been such a good friend to Liz this year. I'm sure glad she'll have you around this winter."

Jean stiffened for a split second, surprised by the unexpected embrace. But then, unable to resist, she discreetly turned her face to the small pool above his collarbone and inhaled, just as she'd imagined doing moments earlier. His skin, unlike his shirt, smelled of soap and faint musk.

"Let's get these heifers back," he said and released her. "I need to finish the milking."

"Right," Jean said quickly.

As Tommy and Jean opened the doors to get in, an ear-splitting shriek ripped through the air and she and Tommy both jumped. They turned to the small grove of trees lining the west edge of the field a few yards away.

"What is that?" Tommy whispered, his eyes wide.

Goose pimples broke out along Jean's arms and neck. She knew the sound immediately. She tipped her glasses to the end of her nose, the cracked lens warping her line of vision.

"It's a barn owl." She pointed to a high branch in a half-dead oak tree. "There."

Tommy narrowed his eyes and craned his neck, searching. "I see it!" he finally said. "It looks like a damn monkey."

Jean shaded her eyes against the bright morning sun. "They usually only come out at night."

"Then why is that one out during the day?"

"It's probably got a nest of hungry babies somewhere and needs to find food."

"It gives me the creeps. Have you ever seen one in the daytime before?"

Jean nodded, still staring under the visor of her hand at the ghostly bird.

"Once," she whispered with a shudder. "A white owl in daylight; it's a bad omen."

CHAPTER 14

Spring, 1953

It was all a blur: their hasty courtship, brief engagement, and small, thrown-together wedding the following spring at the Chickering United Methodist Church. Jean Gillman officially became Jean Krenshaw on a cold and wet March afternoon in front of forty-three guests with Reverend Iverson and his hairpiece officiating. She wore a simple white A-line dress and short cap veil, both sewn on her mother's old Singer machine, and Jim wore a suit previously purchased for Eunice's funeral, and met his bride at the end of the aisle with a jelly stain on his tie. Sandy served as Jean's maid of honor and only bridesmaid, and Tommy stood up with Jim as best man. They celebrated with a modest cake-and-punch reception in the fellowship hall and the newlyweds spent two days in a cabin at Lake Winnebago. Immediately upon their return, Jean moved into Eunice's former house with Jim.

Toad had not walked Jean down the aisle for her wedding nor given her away, as he had already left Chickering and moved to another rental farm somewhere in the far northwest corner of the state near the Minnesota border. Engaged to Jim by the time her father departed, Jean had stayed with Walt and Bonnie until the wedding. She never saw her father again. He died the following winter after he caught pneumonia and his lungs failed. She'd arranged a respectable funeral, made sure he was buried next to her mother in Cold Spring, and quickly moved on with the business of her life. You lose the light when you chase the shadows, her mother used to say.

Around the same time Toad left Chickering, during the muddy weeks of the winter thaw, Beatrice took a tumble in her yard and broke a hip. She moved to Janesville with one of her unmarried daughters to recover, and died peacefully in her sleep a short time later. Heart attack, the doctor said, but Jim and Tommy said it was from a broken heart that never healed after the death of her beloved sister. Tommy immediately moved into her house, and the brothers took the helm of the farm at last.

Another major event occurred during the spring thaw: Larry's conception. Jean was fairly sure it happened during a particularly frisky night in the milk house shortly after their wedding when she'd brought Jim his dinner. She had not entered their marriage with any kind of *that* experience, make no mistake, and was quite surprised to find doing *that* with her husband was almost nice, if not a little embarrassing. He was gentle and patient with her and had been in an especially sweet mood on the night in question, and Jean was grateful that her first child had been conceived with such love. But no doubt Larry's birth date had many Chickering folks discreetly counting backwards on their fingers.

And finally, Jean and Sandy were slowly making their dream of the seamstress shop a reality. Just as they'd planned in Jean's kitchen, they sold canned goods, fresh baked bread and Jean's potato salad at church events and local gatherings. By summer, they had saved nearly $300. Jim often helped, carrying the heavy boxes of mason jars for them, setting up card tables, and Tommy was a frequent customer. Jean and Sandy made a great team, just as Sandy said they would.

But instead of feeling joyous about the inheritance of the farm, her own home, a new baby, and building the seamstress shop, Jean felt increasingly anxious. It was a nagging feeling, like constantly watching the skyline for signs of an incoming storm.

Sometimes, she would wander the rooms of Eunice's former house, now her house, and run her fingertips over the coarse upholstery of the davenport, the smooth oak of the banister and the cool metal surfaces of her appliances, and she would marvel that she now owned things like an electric mixer, a deep freezer, an automatic washer and dryer, and a full set of perfect, matching dishes. And then she would immediately feel panicked, as if she were about to lose it all to something catastrophic, like a fire or tornado.

Jean frequently thought about the moment when she and Sandy had excitedly conceived of the seamstress shop, how she had started to let her mind dream of more from life. Then, how quickly she'd been plunged into hopelessness when she'd discovered the bank notices hidden beneath her father's mattress. The abrupt, emotional changes in direction left her feeling dizzy.

She was most troubled, though, by all the death around her. Her father, then Beatrice. And she was living in Eunice's house, a woman she'd watched die before her very eyes.

She thought about the white owl.

She thought about Eunice's final words.

Curses, like chickens, come home to roost.

But she went on with the business of life, smiling and working and never letting on, all the while nervously checking the sky.

On their one-year wedding anniversary, Jean and Jim celebrated at home with the freezer-burned top of their wedding cake. Jean slid a knife through the cracked and flaky icing. The narrow edges of the frosted yellow rosebuds appeared crystallized and the inside of the cake was hard, despite thawing out on the kitchen counter for a day. Jim skeptically poked the piece Jean served him.

"This looks strange," he said. He leaned down to examine the slice more closely.

"It'll look a little different after being in the freezer for a whole year, but it's fine."

"It even smells funny."

"Would you stop complaining!" she said. "It's tradition, for crying out loud! Everyone does it on their first anniversary."

"Well, I've never heard of it."

Jean held up a forkful of cake. "Here's to year number one."

Jim tapped his fork against hers and they simultaneously closed their mouths around the bites, each chewing slowly, lips pursed. Within seconds, their faces twisted up and they spat their mouthfuls into napkins.

"That was horrible!" Jim cried, reaching for a glass of milk.

Jean nodded her head, wiping the napkin around the inside of her mouth. "Really, really awful."

They both started to laugh. "What do you say we forget about the cake and get right to the presents?" Jim said.

"Sounds good to me." Jean cleared the plates from the table and dumped the remainder of the cake into the garbage. She removed a small wrapped box from her hiding place under the sink and returned to the table. She perched on the edge of her chair, watching intently as he grinned and tore off the paper. He lifted a small leather-bound notepad from the box.

"It's for you to write down tag numbers of the heifers so you don't have to write them on your hand or arm anymore like some tattooed gypsy." She pointed to the pad. "There's even a pen and it's attached so you won't lose it. And it fits right in your front pocket."

Jim ran his hands over the soft dark cover. "I love it," he said and kissed the top of her head.

"First anniversary—paper." Jean pressed her face into the pilled flannel of his shirt, breathing in his now familiar scent of Ivory soap and iodine.

"Okay, now you."

He grabbed her hand and pulled her from the chair, practically dragging her up the stairs in his excitement.

"Slow down!" she whispered. "You'll wake the baby!"

Jim stopped at the door to the narrow anteroom leading up to the attic. "I have a surprise for you." He removed a small skeleton key from his pants pocket and unlocked the glass knob.

Jean stepped inside and her eyes welled with tears. He had moved in the old desk and chair from one of the spare bedrooms and set up her Singer sewing machine. A corkboard dotted with tacks for her patterns hung on one wall and large pegboards were mounted on another for all her spools of thread and scissors. Jim had made her a sewing room.

"What...when did you do this?" She turned in dazed circles.

"Yesterday afternoon while you were in town. I thought you could do a little work here until you and Sandy can the store going."

Jean ran her hands over the shiny top of her sewing machine, which he'd clearly oiled and polished. Her life had become more than she'd ever allowed herself to hope for—a nice home, a child, a prosperous husband who was good to her—and her heart swelled.

She wandered to the small, square window and peered out at the yard and driveway below while Jim chattered about another cabinet he could bring up from the basement for her if she wanted. Outside, Tommy walked into view, carrying a bucket of feed toward the calf huts.

The muscular outline of his shoulders strained against the fabric of his jacket. He paused to switch the heavy bucket to his opposite hand. Jean felt the familiar catch in her stomach at the mere sight of him, and the joyous swell in her heart she'd felt moments before deflated.

She'd worked hard to stuff away those feelings from that

first summer, whittling away at the memory of the day in her father's kitchen when she'd tried to kiss Tommy, until it was down to nothing more than a sliver in her mind. She and Tommy never spoke of it, and over time, he found his way back to his sister-in-law's kitchen just across the driveway to share meals and tease her. They attended church services together every Sunday and she brought him breakfast when he milked the morning shift, just as she did for Jim. And she and Tommy and Sandy started spending time together again, an easy trio once more.

Despite the reminders that she had a good, comfortable life, the anxiousness persisted. She felt like the worm creatures from childhood had returned to swim in her blood, to poison her body and mind, and she fought the urge to constantly check the sky.

"Hey, you listening?" Jim asked.

She glanced at him over her shoulder. "I'm listening. I was just admiring my view."

"I was saying that I could also hang a light right here to make it brighter over the desk if you wanted."

Jean turned back to the window but Tommy was gone.

"Are you happy with it?" Jim asked.

She wiped a smudge from the glass pane. "Yes," she said quietly. "I'm happy."

CHAPTER 15

Christmas, 1954

Jean rummaged through piles of sagging boxes crowding the attic floor in search of missing Christmas decorations. Since Jim had moved everything out of the anteroom the previous spring to create her sewing room, she'd been missing a box of garlands and a nativity set that had once belonged to Beatrice.

She could faintly see her breath in the unheated, chilly attic air and pulled her cardigan tightly across her chest. The naked bulb above her head flickered and she tapped it several times until the weak light reappeared. She pushed on the corner of a heavy wooden trunk to free up another dusty box and opened it. Old farming magazines. She frowned and shoved it aside.

She easily slid another box out from under the eaves and pulled off a strip of brittle, yellowed tape. Inside were old papers belonging to Eunice and her husband—bank statements, woodworking magazines, and a rubber-banded stack of receipts. She hadn't realized some of their belongings were still floating around the house.

She next hoisted up the lid on a large steamer trunk and paused to sneeze after disturbing the thick layer of dust. The air inside smelled musty and a scattering of mold dotted the cloth-lined corners of the lid. Jean picked through the first miscellaneous items: bundles of patchwork squares tied with pieces of ribbon, a box of broken hat pins, several kid gloves missing their mates.

"Jean?" a high voice called from the stairs.

"Up here, Sandy," Jean answered.

Sandy climbed the stairs and stepped gingerly around the scattered boxes to where Jean was kneeling on the floor. "The door was open," she said. "What are you doing up here?"

"Looking for some missing Christmas decorations." Jean shoved a broken rocking chair out of the way.

Sandy crouched next to Jean and inspected the contents of the trunk Jean had been looking at moments earlier. "What is all this?" she asked.

"I think it's some of Jim's Aunt Eunice's old things."

"Eunice Krenshaw," Sandy exhaled, picking up a sparkling hatpin. "What an odd woman."

"What makes you say that?" Jean asked.

"I don't know." Sandy shrugged. "She was just so...*unpleasant* all the time."

"Maybe she had a hard life," Jean said.

"Maybe." Sandy tossed the pin back into the trunk.

Jean closed the lid and secured the latch. Talking about Eunice suddenly made her feel melancholy.

"What decorations are you missing?" Sandy asked. "I'll help you look."

"A box of garland and a nativity set."

Sandy twisted around, surveying the length of the attic. "Where have you already looked?"

"Well," Jean sighed, "I've been through all of those." She pointed to a jumbled stack of boxes ready to topple over. "There's a few boxes really wedged in the corner over there but I'm so tall I can't—"

Before Jean could finish, Sandy was shimmying around the messy piles and under the eaves, like a mole burrowing into the earth. She reached the two small boxes crammed under the lowest section of the roofline.

"You're right, these are really stuck," she grunted, wriggling one of the boxes back and forth until a top flap tore free. "Eureka!" she cried. "This looks like a nativity set to me!"

"Really?" Jean smiled with relief. "The last blasted box, of course."

Sandy stretched and handed the box over to Jean. "Isn't that how it always goes?" she said. She crawled back out of the maze and stood, brushing a smudge of dust from the lapel of her blouse. "I think you'll need a new box, though."

Jean opened the torn flap and found Beatrice's milky white porcelain nativity set in perfect condition. She removed the Joseph and Mary and held them side by side in her palm. She thought about the box of her mother's Christmas decorations she'd had to leave behind during one of the moves with her father, and the melancholy descended again.

"They're beautiful, aren't they?" Jean said sadly.

Sandy touched her shoulder. "Are you okay?" she asked.

Jean looked up and quickly put a smile on her face. "Oh, I'm fine. Just thinking about how much I still have to do to get ready for the holidays. I should really get back downstairs before Larry wakes up from his nap." She tucked the two figurines back inside the nest of newspapers.

"I can help," Sandy said.

Jean pointed to a spot just above Sandy's left ear. "You've got some cobwebs in your hair."

"No spiders, I hope!" Sandy laughed. She unclipped the barrette at the nape of her neck and raked her fingers through her hair.

"Are they gone?" Sandy said.

"Gone," Jean said.

Sandy turned Jean in a small circle. "Now you. There's dust all over the back of your sweater."

Jean slipped her arms out of the cardigan and gave it a couple of hard flicks. As she brushed the back of the cardigan clean with her hand, she realized too late she was standing in her camisole with the scarred skin of her arms and wrists exposed. She hastily tried to put the cardigan back on, but Sandy was already staring, open mouthed and unblinking.

"Jean, what happened to your arms?" she asked.

Jean's mind scrambled to form the rehearsed explanation she always used. "Oh, these?" she said, as casually as she could make her voice sound. "I've been so clumsy my entire life! You wouldn't even believe it!" She waved her hand, trying to appear as convincing as she did when Jim believed, and never doubted, her excuses. "I'm always bumping into things. Accidentally burning myself." She laughed tightly.

Sandy stepped closer. She took Jean's hand into her own and turned it over, exposing a fresh burn that was healing over an existing scar on the inside of Jean's wrist she'd inflicted with a lit match. "Jean," she said softly, "what is this?"

"It's what I said—" she started to protest, but the words caught in her throat. With Sandy's warm skin against her own, she began to shiver and goose pimples rose on her forearms and scalp. The creepy-crawlies, her mother had always called them.

Her speech began to crumble and fail, and tears flooded her eyes. Sandy searched her face for an answer and for the first time in her life, Jean realized how badly she wanted to say it out loud.

"Sometimes," Jean said, her voice quavering, "I just feel so unhappy. And this," she touched the burn on her wrist, "is the only thing that makes me feel better."

Sandy pulled Jean into an embrace. "Oh, Jean," she said. "Whatever could you have to be so unhappy about?"

Jean thought about Tommy and her throat tightened. She wished she were brave enough to tell Sandy everything.

"Please don't tell anyone," she said. "Even Jim doesn't know. He would never understand, so I make up good excuses and he believes them."

"Of course," Sandy said. "Your secret is safe with me."

"Ladies?" a male voice called from the bottom of the

stairs.

Jean and Sandy quickly separated.

"We're up here, Tommy," Sandy answered. "He and I have a little early Christmas present to give you," she whispered. She wiped Jean's face dry with the sleeve of her blouse.

"Are you cooking a separate pie up there?" Tommy said. "'Cause the one down here in the oven is starting to burn."

"We're coming," Jean replied. She slipped her cardigan back on and picked up the box with the nativity set to carry downstairs. "What kind of surprise?"

"You'll see," Sandy said with a wink.

Downstairs, Jean set the nativity scene on the kitchen table as Sandy and Tommy stood together on the opposite side.

"Are you ready to give her the thing?" Sandy asked.

"Yep." He rooted around the front inside pocket of his denim work coat and extracted a rectangular, dark green velvet jewelry box.

"For you," Sandy said. "From me." Tommy nudged her in the ribs with his elbow. "I mean, from us."

Jean took the box and ran her fingers over the worn velvet cover. "What is this?" she asked.

"Just open it."

Jean cracked the lid and gasped. Inside was a small strand of real ivory pearls with a solid gold sunflower clasp.

"Now, before you say no," Sandy put her hand up, "they were my great Aunt Harriet's and I never liked her because she smelled like mothballs and always pinched my cheeks. And I already have a strand of my mother's and no girl needs two pearl necklaces in one lifetime!"

"I can't take these," Jean said. "It's too much." She snapped the lid shut and set the box on the table.

"It's okay." Sandy gently pushed the box back toward her. "I want you to have them. Tommy and I talked about it." She paused. "He told me about what your father did with your mother's pearls."

Jean stared down at the box and blinked away hot tears. It was one of the nicest things anyone had ever done for her. Sandy Weaver, it seemed, was almost too good to be true.

"Thank you," Jean finally managed to say. She swiped at her wet eyes, which were growing red and puffy from all the crying she'd done in one morning.

"You're welcome," Sandy said, her nose bright pink from crying again, too.

"Hey, no tears!" Tommy said. He grabbed Sandy and pulled her and Jean into a hug. The Three Musketeers. For as long as the trio, and the pearls, were Jean's to claim.

CHAPTER 16

September, 1964

In early September, Tommy and Liz hosted a Sunday dinner for the Krenshaw family. When Walt was still alive, Bonnie hosted the dinners, then after his death, Jean took over. But so far Liz had never offered to host a Sunday dinner, and there were no holidays or special occasions to celebrate. They'd never offered to host a Sunday dinner before and there were no holidays or special occasions to celebrate. Tommy and Liz had been vague about their reasons for the gathering, so Jean was immediately suspicious. She had a strange feeling what the announcement was going to be and had been preparing herself since the morning the cattle got out.

Jean stood on their porch flanked by Jim, Bonnie, and the three boys. She cradled a pot of corn on the cob in her hands while Bonnie carried her butter and brown sugar lefse, a traditional Norwegian flatbread. The standard Krenshaw family meal of ham, potatoes, creamed corn casserole and soup was usually Jean's responsibility, but Liz had insisted on preparing the meal herself, and had kept the menu a closely guarded secret.

Liz answered the door wearing a sleeveless, knee-length shift in polka dot print, her hair blown into a long flip. She looked beautiful and fashionable and so oddly out of place standing in the doorway of a farmhouse.

"Benvenuto!" she said. "That's 'welcome' in Italian." Her voice was more cheerful than it had been in recent weeks.

"What do we have here?" Tommy lifted the lid of Jean's pot.

"Corn on the cob," Jean said. "Fresh from my garden."

"Ah, damn! First batch of sweet corn!" Tommy said. "Lizzy was so disappointed that her corn didn't take this year."

Jean made sure to keep her face neutral at the mention of Liz's garden. "Maybe next year she'll have better luck."

Will jostled a glass pie pan in his hands. "My arms are getting tired."

"Just set it down before you drop it and ruin the dessert," Bonnie said, shoving her tray of lefse into Tommy's hands.

A black puppy bounded into the kitchen, stumbling over paws too big for its body, and went right to Jean, sniffing around her feet with small barks and yips. The boys fell to their knees in excited chatter.

"A little gift from Tommy when I wasn't feeling very well," Liz said. "She's a Labrador. I named her Dixie."

"She's so cute!" James said. He was lying on the floor with his nose inches away from Dixie's. "Look! She's licking my fingers!"

Liz bent over with her hands on her knees. "I already taught her a trick this morning. Watch." She extracted a small doggie treat from the wide pocket of her dress and held it above the dog's head. "Dixie! Sit! Sit, Girl!" The dog sniffed at Liz's hand for a moment then promptly dropped her hind legs. Everyone clapped.

"Why can't we ever get a dog?" Will asked, stroking Dixie's ebony coat.

"They're a lot of work," Jean said.

"Oh, but they're so worth it," Liz said. "We've had so much fun with her already."

Dixie was now painfully nipping at Jean's ankles and she discreetly gave the pooch a sharp nudge with her foot. The dog began to howl. Liz led the cowering puppy to a little bed in the corner of the kitchen by tugging on a red bandana tied around Dixie's neck.

"Can we eat before everything gets cold?" Bonnie asked, settling herself at the table before anyone answered.

"Yes, please, everyone, let's sit down," Liz said. She lit half a dozen tapers in a brass candelabrum on the table. "A wedding gift from my aunt and uncle," she said, pointing to the brass centerpiece. "I haven't had a chance to use them yet."

"Beautiful." Jean nodded, choosing a seat between Jim and her mother-in-law. "Is she planning to serve the queen of England, too?" Bonnie said under her breath to Jean. Liz pretended not to hear, though her cheeks reddened slightly.

The dinner party settled around the small dinette set, cobbled together with a shaky card table to accommodate the boys. Jean felt chilled despite the crowded room and candles on a warm September day, and was glad she had worn a light cardigan.

"I thought it would be fun to share a traditional Italian dinner," Liz said. "The kind my mother used to make when I was a little girl." She proudly removed a glass dish from the oven, in what appeared to be several meats of unknown origin. "We call it The Feast of Seven Fishes!"

"There's no ham?" Bonnie asked, incredulously shaking her head. "No mashed potatoes?"

Liz's smile faltered. "Well, it's seven kinds of seafood. There's shrimp, clams with pasta, mussels, scungilli, baccala, which is dried salt cod, calamari, and the big fish is salmon." She pointed to each section of seafood in the pan as she talked.

"Looks great to me, Baby." Tommy patted his wife's bottom and Liz smiled appreciatively as she set the pan in the center of the table.

"What's this one," Bonnie asked, wrinkling her nose. "The cala-what's-who's it?"

"Calamari," Liz said. "It's squid."

"What?" Bonnie barked. "Are you pulling my leg? I'm not eating squid! Where did you even get it?"

Liz bit her lip and momentarily looked as if she were going to cry. "I...it's really very good."

Long ago, Jean had categorized her family members as a different species of tree, like she had with her children and fruit. Jim was an oak, rugged and conventional, Tommy was a sugar maple, everyone's favorite, and Bonnie was a walnut, hearty but sometimes an annoying nuisance. Jean's mother would have been a silver maple, graceful and elegant, her father a prickly Chinese chestnut, while Jean saw herself as a poplar, towering and sturdy. Since the Fourth of July picnic last year, she had been pondering the right tree for Liz. That very moment with the casserole dish of sea treasures making its way around the table, one finally came to her. Liz was a redbud tree, petite and pretty, but mostly ornamental.

After Bonnie led the grace, Liz took her seat next to Tommy and passed around a second platter of baked red peppers and a bowl of broccoli and black olive salad.

"Now what the hell is this?" Bonnie asked.

Liz leaned forward to inspect the contents on Bonnie's fork. "That's the scungilli. It's baked conch."

"Like one of them shells you put up to your ear to hear the ocean?" Larry asked.

"Right. But you eat what's inside the shell," Liz said.

Bonnie switched to her salad instead. Jim was already discreetly picking the black olives out of his.

At the children's table, Jean noticed the boys whispering and smirking over their plates. She watched them from the corner of her eye for a moment, her ability to catch children in the act a well-practiced skill. She quickly spotted the source of their conspiratorial snickering—Larry was using his pocketknife, the controversial birthday gift from his uncle last winter, to stab his fish and eat it off the tip like a spear.

"Larry Thomas Krenshaw, where are your manners at a dinner table? Give that knife to me this instant." Jean snapped her fingers and held her hand out. "You obviously can't handle the responsibility, so hand it over."

Larry raised his hands in self-defense. "I wasn't doing anything!"

Jim set his fork down onto the table. "Give it to your mother, Larry. Now. "

Larry reluctantly handed the knife, handle first, over to Jean. She wiped the blade clean on her napkin before closing it, and slipped it into the pocket of her cardigan.

Tommy shook his head, trying not to smile at his nephew. "I told you to mind your Ps and Qs with that thing, Knucklehead."

Larry scowled and crossed his arms.

"Oh! The bread!" Liz cried and leaped up to open the oven door. She handed a warm tray of bread slices to Tommy and he selected two, each piece dropping like a rock against the china plate. He made it a point to smile at his wife as she watched intently over his shoulder. He buttered the concrete-like surfaces with a grating *scrape scrape* sound that made the entire kitchen shudder.

Dixie had wandered from her corner and was softly whining at Jean's feet under the table. She reached down and scratched at the hard crest between the pup's ears, and Dixie panted and wagged her tail in happy response. Jean slipped a spoonful of the calamari beneath the table. The dog sniffed and ventured a lick, but sneezed and turned away, trotting back to her bed. Jean thought she might like this Dixie after all.

Tommy excused himself from the table but returned moments later with a long, green velvet jewelry box in his hand.

"Well," he said. "I've been waiting to give this special present to Lizzie until we were ready to share our big news."

Jean's heartbeat skipped.

The green velvet box. It couldn't be. She held her breath.

Liz pried the lid open and held up a string of pale white pearls. "Oh, Tommy!" she gasped. "They're beautiful."

Tommy opened the clasp, the telltale gold sunflower clasp of Sandy's pearl necklace. Exactly as Jean remembered it the day she'd given it back to Tommy. The mere sight of the necklace, the gleaming opaque balls, smooth as glass, set off a blooming explosion of tiny pinpricks over her scalp, down her back, and across her arms until the fine dark hairs stood on end.

Liz stood as Tommy laid the pearls around her delicate neck, and she fingered them at the base of her throat. She bent forward slightly and pulled her hair over her shoulder, out of the way. Beneath the table, Jean shoved her clenched fists into the pockets of her sweater and felt the hard shape of Will's knife. She loosened her fingers and withdrew the cold metal from her pocket where she carefully opened the blade, mindful to keep her expression steady and engaged in the conversation. She slowly inched the hem of her skirt up until her right thigh was exposed, and pressed the cold steel blade to the warm inner skin. As she was about to cut, she watched a lock of Liz's hair fall free, directly over the candelabrum. Jean hesitated, the knife still poised against her skin. The weak flame of a taper licked the tips of Liz's dark strands for a split second before erupting into a small ball of fire on the side of her head. She screamed and batted at the flame creeping toward her face and ear. In a flash of movement, Tommy swatted the flame out with his bare hand.

Stunned silence paralyzed the room. A sickening acrid smell filled the air.

"Holy shit," Tommy finally breathed. "Are you alright?" He laid his hand against her abdomen.

Jean closed the blade of the knife and quickly slipped it back into her pocket.

Liz managed a weak nod and wiped at the ashen tear

streaks on her cheek. "My hair!" she wailed, feeling the singed edges around her earlobe. Amazingly, she had suffered no burns but for the missing chunk of hair, giving her head a lopsided appearance. Jim wet a towel in the sink and handed it to Liz.

"Well," Tommy said, his voice quavering and uncharacteristically rattled. "I was working my way up to telling you all that come next April, my beautiful wife is going to make me a father."

"Oh, Tommy!" Bonnie cried, clasping her hands together. "That's wonderful news!"

"Congratulations, little brother." Jim stood and slapped Tommy on the back, then kissed Liz on the cheek. "Glad to see you two didn't wait."

Tommy put his arm around Liz's shoulder and pulled her close to his hip. "We've known for several weeks. It was a bit of a shock at first, but we're over the moon, right, Baby?"

"Of course," Liz said. She glanced at Jean and the flickering candles cast strange, moving shadows over her eyes.

Jean stood and walked around the table, thinking of the little container of pills she'd found in the shoebox the day Liz had moved into the house.

"Congratulations," she said, embracing Liz in a stiff hug. "What a happy surprise that must have been."

CHAPTER 17

September, 1964

"That was quite a night," Jim said, once they were home from dinner and had tucked the boys in bed.

"Mmm-hmm," Jean was rearranging items in the refrigerator to make room for the leftover pie and desserts. She kept her back to her husband. She could feel the remnants of the evening on her skin, like an unpleasant layer of dirt and oil absorbing slowly through her pores.

Jim dropped onto a chair to remove his shoes. "Isn't it great about Tommy and Liz, though?"

"I forgot my pot," Jean said.

"What?" Jim shook his head, confused.

"I left my pot on their counter."

"I'll get it tomorrow."

She turned around to face him. "I'll need it first thing in the morning. We're having roast. I can't make roast without my large pot."

He sighed. "I'll get it in the morning."

Jean waved her hand. She glanced out the window and slipped on her shoes. "Their lights are still on. I'll just get it myself."

She tromped the path of worn grass, anxious to talk to Tommy alone. She needed to ask him about Sandy's pearls, to hear him explain why he'd decided to give them to Liz. Just seeing the pearls again after all this time had left her feeling rattled and wrung out.

As she reached the porch door and lifted her hand to knock, the sound of a muffled cry stopped her. She stepped around the corner and peeked through the lighted front window, covered only by sheer curtains. There, in the center of the living room floor, Tommy lay naked on his back with Liz atop him, straddled and riding, her hips rocking, eyes closed. She threw her head back, creating a wild rainbow of dark hair. The pearls clung to her arched, smooth throat. Tommy murmured something inaudible and reached up to cup her full breasts.

Jean's heavy breath made a foggy, wet circle on the glass. She felt dizzy and began to shiver, chilled once again. She slowly backed away and missed the first step of the porch. She twisted her ankle and fell onto her side as sharp pain stabbed through her ribs. She regained her footing and hurried back to the house.

Inside, Jean went straight upstairs to the bathroom and locked the door. She undressed slowly, her fingers stiff and unyielding as she unbuttoned her sweater. She left her clothing in a messy heap on the floor and stood in her white panties, trying to catch her breath.

Her skin felt hot like she was running a fever, so she took her temperature with a glass thermometer. While waiting with the thermometer pursed between her lips, she caught a glimpse of her flushed reflection in the mirror—her small, sagging breasts, the rippled lines across her belly and padded hips marking each one of her pregnancies. The image of the white pearls against Liz's smooth, dark skin flashed through her mind. She turned her back on the mirror.

Jean removed the thermometer and held it up to the light above the medicine chest. 98.1—normal. She turned off the light and lowered herself to the floor, sitting naked on the bath mat with her back pressed against the cold porcelain of the tub. She drew her knees to her chest.

She blinked at the darkness before her and thought of the morning she'd given the pearl necklace back to Tommy, after the fateful trip to Chicago with Sandy.

The more time passed, the fuzzier some details about the trip became. There were certain things she could no longer recall—if the cab driver had played the radio, the name of the motel they stayed in that night, what the ambulance drivers looked like. But some things refused to leave her, always lurking in the dank, musty corners of her memory, like the woman's dirty housecoat, the smell of the woman's kitchen, and the image of Sandy's long blonde hair fanned out across the backseat of the cab.

Sometimes, though not very often, Jean dreamed about a ghostly version of Sandy where her face was a white mask and there were dark, empty holes where her eyes should be, and Jean would awaken with a start, her heart pounding, the sheets damp with sweat.

"Jean?" Jim knocked on the door and startled her. "Are you coming to bed?"

"In a minute," she called.

She closed her eyes and leaned her head back against the edge of the tub. She sensed a subtle shift happening in the tenuous stability of her inner workings. It was as if the scale of her life she'd so painstakingly balanced since the Chicago trip—endlessly stacking weights and counterweights to each side—had suddenly become lopsided since Liz's arrival and gone into free fall.

Jean reached up and switched on the light. She rooted through the pocket of her sweater until she found Will's pocketknife once more. This time, when she put the blade to the thin skin of her inner thigh, skin so thin and pale she could see a roadmap of blue veins just below the surface, she cut. Just a few inches, until the knife separated the flesh and produced a satisfying sting. She leaned her head back against the edge of the tub and closed her eyes once more, savoring the small waves of pain, each one rolling across her skin and through her nerve endings with different tempos and intensities, like notes of music. She let the blood rise and pool, then spill over and run down her thigh. She stanched it with a tissue just before it dripped off her skin and onto the bathmat, and then covered the cut with a small bandage. She returned the knife to the pocket of her cardigan.

In the bedroom, Jim lay beneath the bedcovers. Jean rummaged through her dresser drawer until she found a soft flannel nightgown usually reserved for frigid winter nights, the floral one with a pretty lace collar that Jim had given her one Christmas, which nearly covered her from head to toe. She quickly slipped it over her head.

"Did you get the pot?" Jim asked through a long yawn.

Jean picked up his dirty clothes from the floor and stuffed them into the hamper. "They were already asleep."

"I'll get it first thing tomorrow morning then."

She removed her glasses and lowered herself into bed, the old metal springs protesting against her weight, and rolled over onto her side.

"You're sore at me for not getting the pot tonight."

"No," Jean finally said.

Jim moved close behind and placed a hand on her shoulder with a light squeeze, his little signal to let her know he wanted to make love. She moved onto her back and allowed him to clumsily push her gown up to her stomach. He slid her white panties down, the elastic waistband snapping her hips when he lost his grip.

"Be careful," she said, "I got careless with the razor in the tub this morning and have a little cut on my leg."

He ran his fingers from her knee up to her thigh, until they found the bandage. He gently laid his palm over the cut.

"Poor Jean," he whispered, "always so clumsy."

As Jim settled on top of her, his weight sending white hot currents of pain through her leg, Jean fought the urge to reach up and slap him.

CHAPTER 18

January, 1955

Jean lugged yet another heavy basket of soiled sheets and blankets down to the basement to be washed. Little Larry had caught the flu from one of the Hansen boys in the church nursery and had soiled through his cloth diapers every night for four nights in his feverish sleep, bless his heart. The piles of smelly laundry never stopped. So many Jean had lost count. Not a promising start to the New Year.

It wasn't yet seven in the evening and Jean could barely keep her eyes open. Larry was finally asleep and it was all she wanted to do herself. She'd managed a few hours of dozing each night, up and down a dozen times with the baby for one thing or another. She hadn't bothered to wake Jim for help since it was his week to milk the morning shift, rising at 3:30 before sunrise. Farm, God, then family, she knew.

Exhausted, she mistakenly dumped two cups of Borax soap instead of one into the metal basin. She sighed and sagged against the machine. The porch door slammed upstairs, followed by footsteps across the kitchen floor. Thinking Jim must have finished chores early and was in for the night to help her, Jean nearly burst into tears of relief. The basement door opened a crack and a weak shaft of light illuminated the stairs.

"Jean?" a small voice called.

Jean straightened. "Down here, Sandy." She cranked the dial on the machine.

Sandy's galoshes, wet from the snow, squeaked on the wooden stairs as she made her way down slowly, taking care not to slip.

"Hi," Jean said. "Beware. We're contagious around here." She started unpinning a set of dry sheets from the clothesline that stretched from one end of the basement to the other.

Sandy unbuttoned her gray pea coat and removed her wool hat. Her hair fell in a tangled ponytail down her back.

"Tommy said you've had a rough week," she said. "Thought I'd come see if you needed any help."

Jean managed a weary smile. "That's nice of you."

Sandy stepped under the harsh overhead light and Jean noticed at once how pale and wan she looked. Her lips were so dry the corners of her mouth were cracked.

"Don't tell me you're sick too?" Jean asked.

Sandy shook her head. "No. Nothing like that." She stood on her toes and looked out the narrow basement window. "Can you believe it's supposed to snow again?" she said. "I'm so ready for winter to be over."

"Unfortunately," Jean replied with a wooden clothespin pursed between her lips, "We have several months to go. Oh, that reminds me. You left your black gloves here the other day. The nice leather ones."

Sandy nodded and brushed stray hairs from her eyes. She started folding a basket of clean towels on top of the folding table. As she held up the edges of a towel, her hands visibly trembled.

Jean dumped out a pile of sheets and studied the girl's face. "Are you sure you're okay?"

"I'm fine!" Sandy said quickly, her voice tight, high-pitched. "Honest." She looked at Jean and forced a smile. "I'm just tired, that's all. I've been helping my mother bake all day for the church fund-raiser."

Jean stacked the folded towels in the basket. She unpinned a quilt from the line and carefully aligned two corners. Sandy did the same at the opposite end and they walked toward each other until their ends touched. Standing only inches apart, Jean noticed Sandy's puffy eyes and red nose. Jean added the quilt to the basket.

"Have you been crying?" she said.

Sandy's face instantly crumbled with tears.

Jean led the girl to the narrow bottom step of the stairs where they sat, shoulders pressed to one another.

"It's okay," Jean said, rubbing her back. "You can tell me. My mother always used to say a trouble shared is a trouble halved."

Sandy pulled her knees to her chest and lowered her head. "Oh, Jean!" she cried. "I'm with...you know...Gosh, I can't even say it!" She looked at Jean and the naked bulb hanging directly above cast queer shadows over her eyes, creating dark, empty sockets.

"I'm in a family way," she whispered.

Jean's mouth opened. Her eyes instinctively moved to Sandy's middle. "What? Are you sure?"

"I just found out a few days ago." Sandy hiccupped, twisting the large top button on her coat. "I lied to my parents and told them I was spending the day with you making bread for another sale but I went to a doctor in Janesville instead because I missed my cycle last month and I never miss and I've been feeling really sick, so I saw this doctor and he told me it's six weeks. I'm six weeks." She broke into sobs.

"Oh, no," Jean said. She drew Sandy's head down to her lap and stroked her hair.

"It happened only a few times, I swear!" Sandy cried against Jean's legs. "I know it's a sin but it felt right because we love each other and I would never be with anyone unless I loved him. But my parents, oh, Jean, my parents! They'll never forgive me!"

Sandy bolted upright and started pacing the confined length of the basement, twisting the top button on her coat again, visibly straining the crisscrossed thread. "I thought that maybe if we got married right away and tell everyone about the baby after," she said, "then there's not much they can do about it, right?"

Jean nodded in agreement, though it seemed as if Sandy were talking it through with only herself.

"But then I started thinking about the seamstress shop and how close we are to making it happen and I don't know if I really want to get married because if we do get married I'll always wonder if he only married me for the baby and if he feels like I trapped him."

"Sandy, who is—"

"The doctor told me about this place," she continued, her speech almost frantic, "where I could go until the baby is born and then put it up for adoption." She slapped her hands against her sides. "But my parents! I'd still have to tell my parents. My father will disown me!" Sandy whirled around and searched Jean's face with wide, panicked eyes. "What do you think I should do? Say something, please!"

Jean stood and gathered Sandy's cold, trembling hands into her own in an attempt to calm the girl. "Sandy, slow down. First of all, who is the father?"

Sandy's expression faltered. "Jean," she said, her voice cracking. "It's Tommy."

Jean flinched as if Sandy had struck her. She took a step back, her hand outstretched, groping the air for the stairs. She dropped hard onto her tailbone and became singularly aware of her heart pounding behind her breast, as if it were trying to beat its way out of her body. All sound fell away but for the whishing blood through her veins. She was startled to feel her own hand at the base of her neck, her cold fingers a shock against her hot skin.

Of course.

"I'm so sorry!" Sandy said. "I wasn't trying to keep it a secret from you or anything and I really wanted to tell you when it started last summer but I didn't know how."

Jean's mind immediately began to dissect the moments she'd spent in Sandy and Tommy's presence, reexamining every gesture, every facial expression, every interaction with a critical eye. Like revisiting a book read long ago, the story morphed before her, developing a deeper, more complex plot. She now saw the constant glances and smiles across the table between Tommy and Sandy during lunches in Jean's kitchen, the shared chocolate ice cream cone from Dawson's during a trip into town, the movie in Janesville when she thought for just a moment she saw them holding hands. She recalled a Sunday evening when Sandy had offered to take a warm plate of dinner out to the barn for Tommy, and how, when she'd failed to return after nearly an hour, Jean had gone out after her and interrupted what looked to have possibly been an embrace.

And the pearl necklace, a gift they'd given her, together.

Of course.

Sandy half coughed, half sobbed into her fist. "I'm so sorry for not telling you, Jean. You have to believe me. I know you told me private things and a few times I thought maybe you knew and were just being polite by not saying anything."

Jean thought of the many times when Sandy had come to the house to visit and how she'd asked where Tommy was, what Tommy was doing, when was Tommy coming in for lunch, and suddenly their friendship felt spoiled. She felt used. There had never been a trio. There had only been a duo, and she had been playing the third wheel.

Of course.

And really, she'd known. She'd known all along. She'd just chosen not to believe.

Her eyes moved from Sandy's abdomen up her breasts, to her neck and lips, imagining what Tommy would have done in any one of those stolen moments, the loving touches and caresses, the words whispered into her ears. She heard their hushed promises to each other, vows to keep their love a secret from the world, from Jean. They would've talked about her in those intimate moments, said her name and agreed to keep her ignorant of the affair. When her back was turned, there would've been knowing glances, secret smiles and winks, all while she'd kept happily playing the fool.

She clenched her fists, digging her ragged nails into the palms of her hands.

Sandy dropped to her knees and buried her face in Jean's lap. "I'm so scared. Please, tell me what to do."

Jean vaguely heard Sandy's plea, muffled by the blood still pounding in her eardrums. The skin on her palms began to burn and yet she kept squeezing, pushing the nails deeper, wanting to break skin and feel blood. All at once, she smelled her mother, sweeping into the Clermont house wearing her best dress suit after getting caught in a rainstorm one morning, reincarnated by the scent of Sandy's damp pea coat and hot, perspiring skin. Jean breathed the mixture of damp wool and sweet brown sugar, and nearly wept with the weight of it all.

"If Tommy marries me, I want it to be for love, not obligation," Sandy said. She pawed at Jean's legs like a mewling, newborn kitten, shaking and blindly searching for its mother.

Sandy wrenched her hands away and resumed her nervous pacing.

"But then I keep thinking that if there were no baby," she said, "then maybe you and I and the seamstress shop could still have a chance. Maybe even Tommy and I would still have a chance." She stopped abruptly, as if she'd run headfirst into some invisible wall. Her eyes grew unfocused and she swayed.

"I, I know a girl," she said quietly. "From school. Our senior year. She got into trouble and went to see a man in Chicago and he took care of it."

Slowly, coming back to Sandy's voice, Jean opened her hands and looked down. Four deep crescent gouges marred each palm. The washing machine swished and gurgled. Larry began to cry, his small, hollow wail carrying through the intestines of the house.

"I could call her," Sandy said. "Ask how to get in touch with this man. Chicago is less than three hours away. I could tell my parents we're going out of town for the weekend to sell our jars at some festival or something."

She sat down next to Jean and her eyes welled with tears once more. "Will you go with me? I don't think I could do it alone."

Jean looked into Sandy's eyes, those blue crepe satin eyes, and inhaled her friend's scent once more that she'd come to know and love.

Her mind played another possible stolen late night scene: Tommy's car windows fogged over from heated breath, buttons hastily unfastened, stockings tangled, whispers, *I love you, I love you.*

Jean had been wrong. Sandy was too good to be true.

"Yes," she said finally, "I'll go with you."

Sandy exhaled and wiped her face dry. "I'll need money," she said.

Jean reached out and tucked a lock of hair behind Sandy's ear. "You can use the money we've saved for the seamstress shop," she said, her voice steady now. "If you need it."

"Really?" Sandy said. She pinned Jean's arms down in a crushing hug. "Thank you!"

Jean limply lifted her arms to hug Sandy back.

Out of the frying pan into the fire, her mother used to say.

CHAPTER 19

February 10, 1955

Two weeks to the day after Sandy's revelation in the basement, Jean drove most of the Route 14 trip to Chicago before sunrise as Sandy slept in the seat next to her. They stopped only once, in Harvard, Illinois, for a bathroom break and to gas up the car, and reached the northern city limits in just under three hours as the sun was cresting the horizon. Jean had driven cautiously, her arms tense at the nine and three position, watching her speedometer, and making sure to use her turning signals. They were to be in front of Chester's Deli in Arlington Heights no later than 8:30, the man had said. "Ed" had to be at work by ten and if they were even one minute late, he would leave. He was very clear on this point when Sandy spoke to him on the phone in Jean's kitchen.

Jean, feeling tired and achy, squinted against the bright sun at the names on road signs ahead of her, reading them aloud to herself as she made turns according to the directions Sandy had scribbled down on a piece of paper. Left on Dundee, right on Grove, right on Hintz. She'd never been to Chicago before. The largest city Jean had ever visited was Madison during a weekend dairy convention with Jim last summer, and he'd done all the driving. The traffic in Chicago was a far cry from the traffic in Chickering, which boasted only two stoplights in the entire town.

Sandy was now awake and staring out the window, her hands folded stiffly in her lap, and she offered no navigational assistance. She wore a plain gray wool dress that washed out the color of her skin. Their story for everyone had been detailed and plausible: they were going to take two days and drive to several little towns along Route 14 to sell their jars to interested shops. It was a good lie, Jean thought, because the most efficient falsehoods pepper in as much truth as possible. They really were going to sell jars to interested shops in Walworth, Emerald City, and Janesville on the way home from Chicago, and the trunk of Jean's car was loaded with several boxes of apple butter, jelly, fruit preserves and sweet tomato sauce, which had become their biggest seller. And Jean had arranged for them to stay the night in a little motel in Janesville so they wouldn't have to drive home in the dark, a plan both Jim and Sandy's parents agreed was a good idea, but was really arranged so Sandy could have the night to recover before going home. It was startling to Jean what a gifted architect she'd become at deception.

Jean slowed the car to study the business fronts lining the narrow street.

"There's Chester's Deli," she said, pointing to a peeling black-and-white sign missing the dot to the "i." She parallel parked between a bread truck and a taxicab and cut the engine. Her watch read 8:18. They had over ten minutes to spare.

"That was an easy enough trip," Jean said, stretching her legs. She glanced around the neighborhood. "I'm glad I stuck to Highway 14."

Sandy didn't respond and continued to stare out the window at the people bustling up and down the sidewalk.

"Do you want me to go in and get us some coffee?"

Sandy shook her head and started chewing on her thumbnail.

Jean closed her eyes and rubbed her temples with her fingertips. Her head was throbbing. She'd had no appetite that morning, waking with a sour knot in her stomach after tossing and turning all night.

There was a loud knock on her window and Jean jumped. A startled cry escaped from Sandy. A short, balding man stared at them, a burning cigarette pinched between his thumb and index finger. He impatiently gestured for Jean to roll down her window.

She reluctantly cranked the handle. "Yes?"

"I'm Ed," he said. "Get in the cab." He pointed to the taxi parked in front of them, the motor running.

"Oh," she said, glancing at Sandy. "We—"

Ed didn't wait for her to finish and walked back to his vehicle, slamming the driver's door.

"I, I guess we should..." Jean gathered her purse and buttoned her coat. "Are you ready?"

Sandy's face grew more pale as she stared wide-eyed at the dented fender of the yellow cab. Jean started to open her door but stopped, looking hard at Sandy.

"Do you still want to do this?" she asked. For a split second, despite all the planning and arranging and the long drive, she wanted Sandy to say no so they could turn around and go home. But yet, just as strongly, Jean wanted her to say yes and get out of the car.

Still gnawing on her fingernail, Sandy finally nodded her head and they both climbed out of Jean's Buick, slowly, taking their time to secure the locks on the doors. They inched toward the battered taxicab as Ed gestured to the back seat. He revved the sputtering engine to keep it from dying.

"Now put your heads down," Ed barked once they were inside.

"What? Why?" Jean said.

"Just do it or the deal is off. It's for my own protection."

Sandy immediately flopped over, her blonde hair fanning out on the seat. Jean scrunched herself into a fetal position, resting her head on the crook of her arm, her heart pounding just below her breast. The worn upholstery smelled of cigarette smoke and dirty sweat socks.

The cab lurched forward and Ed lit another cigarette, smoking with the windows mercilessly rolled up. It felt as if they were going in circles and Jean quickly became nauseous. She tried to look over at Sandy, but the girl had curled herself into a ball with her hands over her head, as if practicing for a tornado drill. She wondered what was going through Sandy's mind. Jean herself couldn't hold any thoughts beyond whether or not Ed was going to rob and murder them.

The cab finally jerked to a stop after a dizzying amount of time had passed. Ed cut the engine and ordered the women to get out. When Jean and Sandy finally sat up, blinking and disoriented, they saw the backside of a dilapidated row house. The cab was parked on a steep drive and when Jean tried to open the door to exit, it banged shut against her knee. She gasped and rubbed the flowering bruise just under her skin.

Inside, a gaunt woman wearing a faded floral housecoat greeted them in the dingy, bare kitchen.

"Pay the woman." Ed gestured to her and disappeared through a doorway covered by a bed sheet nailed to the wall.

The woman held out her hand. Sandy pulled her small wallet from her coat pocket and extracted five wrinkled twenty-dollar bills. The woman folded the money in half and slipped it into the strap of her brassiere.

"In there," she said to Sandy, pointing to the sheet-covered room. "Put your coat on the chair and take off your panties. And you," she turned to Jean, "wait here." She pulled out a metal chair at the kitchen table, the legs scraping loudly across the warped floorboards.

Jean sank onto the cold seat and clutched her purse to her chest. The woman pulled the sheet back and beckoned Sandy inside. Jean could see a small lamp illuminating a wooden table and metal pail underneath. Ed was bent over a TV tray, mixing a liquid in a bowl. An iodine-like chemical smell drifted into the kitchen.

Sandy turned to Jean then, her hands pushed deep into the pockets of her coat. "See you in a little bit," she said. Her eyes were wide and seemed to be pleading with Jean, *Stop me. Don't let me do this.*

But Jean didn't know what else to say, so she said, "Good luck."

Sandy lowered her head and followed the woman into the room. The woman dropped the hanging sheet and Sandy disappeared.

Jean perched on the edge of the chair and rubbed her tender kneecap. She could hear Ed talking to Sandy, his voice low but sharp, and see their shadows move back and forth behind the sheet, like a puppet show. Jean closed her eyes and laid her palm against her sweaty forehead, surprised by the hotness of her skin.

"Scoot to the end of the table," Jean clearly heard Ed say.

Jean tried to take a deep breath and unbuttoned her heavy coat. Her clothes beneath were already damp with perspiration. She mopped the back of her neck with a tissue from her purse and laid her head on the table, but immediately sat up. The table was sticky and a plate of moldy bread just inches from her face only made her feel sicker.

This is wrong, her mind screamed. *We shouldn't be here.*

Jean leaped to her feet and reached for the curtain to tell Sandy she'd changed her mind, that they were making a terrible mistake, but stopped, startled by a small pair of eyes staring at her from a darkened doorway. A little boy crouched on the bottom step of a set of stairs. He was barefoot and wore baggy pants with two large holes in the knees. His gnarled hair fell over his ears, and when he smiled at her, he was missing his front two teeth.

"Mama?" he called softly to the other room. The sheet snapped open and the woman appeared.

"I told you to wait upstairs," she said in a firm tone.

"But I'm so hungry," the boy whispered.

"Go on." She shooed him away. "Just a bit longer. We'll buy food when the people leave."

The woman closed the stairwell door and turned to Jean. "That's it. She can get up in about ten minutes. Ed will drive you back to your car."

Jean slumped onto the chair, numb. It was already done. She tried not to look inside the room as Ed drew the sheet open and hooked it on a nail. He switched off the lamp and wiped his hands on a towel. Jean caught another whiff of something strong, iodine or antiseptic. Like the teat dip Jim used on the heifers. She glimpsed Sandy lying on a bare wooden kitchen table, her bent legs covered by a dingy white sheet, arms resting stiffly at her sides.

"She'll start to bleed soon and probably expel it some-time tonight," the woman said. "The bleeding will stop after a week or so. Use a hot water bottle for the pain but no aspirin 'cause that'll make her bleed worse. I gave her a few pads. If she fills more than one an hour, she'll have to see a doctor." The woman loomed over Jean. "But you tell them she had a miscarriage and you don't say a word about us. Understood?"

Jean nodded and shrank deeper onto the chair.

After ten minutes had passed, the woman brought Sandy back into the kitchen, clutching her balled-up coat to her chest. She was trembling and had missed several of the buttons on her dress. Jean slipped an arm around her waist to help her out to the car. Huddled down in the backseat of the taxicab just like before, Sandy began to shiver, cradling her abdomen.

Ed drove them to their car in Arlington Heights and left them in front of the deli without another word. Jean helped Sandy into the back of her Buick where Sandy stretched out, propping her head up with her coat. She was still very chalky and trembling.

"Are you okay back there?" Jean asked as she started the ignition.

"Yeah," Sandy said weakly. "I'm just going to sleep for a while."

"We'll be in Janesville soon," Jean said. "And you can take a nice hot bath at the motel."

"Okay." Sandy nodded and closed her eyes.

They left Arlington Heights and Jean retraced their earlier journey on Route 14. She made quick stops in Walworth and Emerald City as planned, where she sold several boxes of jars to storeowners while Sandy continued to sleep in the backseat.

By the time they arrived in Janesville shortly before dinner, Sandy was bleeding heavily. Jean quickly checked into their motel, a cheap, rundown place close to the highway, and helped Sandy to one of the double beds in the small room. She was in pain by then, and cried and clutched her abdomen, unable to even stand up straight. Jean removed Sandy's heavy wool dress and stockings, which she had completely sweated through, so she would be comfortable in her silk slip. She wiped Sandy's brow with a cold, damp washcloth and tried to get her to eat bites of bread from the small loaf Jean had packed, or sips of water from a plastic cup, but Sandy refused. Finally, Jean just sat on the bed next to her and stroked her hair, comforted her, told her everything was going to be okay, it would all be over soon.

After a few hours, Sandy's skin began to change from pale, to white, and finally to ashen. Her sweat soaked the bed sheets even though she was shivering so hard at times her teeth chattered. She cried and begged Jean to make the pain stop. After she bled through the last pad the woman had given her, Jean started using motel towels in desperation.

"Sandy," Jean said, trying to control her rising panic, "I think you need to go to the hospital."

Sandy moaned and shook her head.

"Listen to me," Jean persisted. "Something's wrong. There's too much blood." Her voice grew thick as her eyes filled with fearful tears. "I don't know what to do."

Jean picked up the telephone on the nightstand and started to dial for an ambulance, but Sandy grabbed her wrist and wrenched the receiver from her hand.

"Don't," Sandy said. "Please. A hospital...they'll call my parents."

Jean tried to wrestle the phone back but Sandy held tight with surprising strength.

"I'm begging you," she said. "Give it a little more time. I'm starting to feel...a bit better." She attempted a weak smile. "Please."

Jean looked at the pleading expression on Sandy's face and felt her resolve begin to wane. She let go of the phone and cradled her head in her hands, trying to collect herself for a moment.

"Okay," Jean finally said. "Just for a little while."

Sandy relinquished the receiver and Jean hung it up.

"I'm glad you're here," Sandy murmured. "I'm glad I'm not alone."

"I'm glad you're not alone, too," Jean said. She pushed a tangled knot of hair from Sandy's face.

After a while, Jean hoisted Sandy out of the bed and dragged her to the bathroom. She laid her in the empty porcelain tub where it was easier to clean her and manage the endless flow of blood. She propped a pillow behind Sandy's head and covered her with a sheet.

"This is just for a little while," Jean said, "and then I'm calling an ambulance if you don't get any better."

Sandy nodded and closed her eyes. "A little while."

Exhausted, Jean collapsed onto the floor next to the tub. She glanced at Sandy and thought that her color looked a tiny bit better since moving her into the bathroom. Her breathing seemed deeper, steadier. Maybe they would get through this without having to go to the hospital after all.

Jean painfully stretched her leg. Her knee ached from

where the car door had slammed into it. She was as physically and emotionally wrung out as she had ever been.

She felt so strange. Light-headed. Detached from her body. Her neck itched with fire.

Her eyes grew heavy and she closed them, intending to rest for just a few minutes.

CHAPTER 20

February 12, 1955

Jean was dreaming of fire.

She was lying on the bathroom floor of the motel with a thick blanket of black smoke pinning her down as bright flames danced closer to her from the doorway. She coughed and tried to lift her head but she was too weak and couldn't breathe. The heat singed her arms and hands when she pushed herself up and reached out to slam the door shut. She recoiled from a snarling flame, her back pressing against the cool porcelain of the tub. She turned and draped her arms over the side, groping for Sandy, crying out for her friend. She felt a leg, a cold hand. Jean shook her shoulder, pulled on her arm, tried to lift her, slapped her face, but Sandy didn't move. The flames inched closer and Jean fanned the smoke from her face, pleading, but, Sandy remained lifeless, her head lolled to the side, her eyes half-open and dull. The heat became unbearable, singeing Jean's hair, scorching her back, her legs. Her feet began to incinerate, turn to ash, and she screamed and begged for mercy.

She jerked awake with a small cry. She lay in a tangle of sheets damp with her own sweat. Bright morning sun glowed through the windows. She blinked, rubbed her face, blearily looked around and saw the comforts of her own bedroom. Her thundering heartbeat slowed and eyes grew heavy once more with drowsy relief. There was no fire. No smoke. She was home. She was safe.

She laid the back of her hand over her hot, clammy forehead. She tried to roll over and a sharp pain splintered through her knee. Her eyes snapped back open.

Sandy, lying in the motel bathtub.

The white sheet covering her body, saturated in dark crimson.

Her dull eyes.

The uniformed men in the ambulance car.

The doctor in the Janesville hospital with his clipboard of questions, his sympathetic hand on her shoulder.

Then the long, silent drive back to Chickering, alone.

Each image assaulted her like blows to the chest.

Sandy.

Jean clenched her eyes closed, drew her head back against the pillow, her spine painfully arching, fists pushing into the mattress, and released a long, animalistic howl that felt like it would tear her throat in two.

Jim burst into the room and tried to wrestle her down but she pounded on his chest, clawed at his face, fought the sheets. He pinned her arms to her sides, whispering in her ear, *it's okay, it's over, you're home now.*

Doctor Cleary came. He held her hot, limp wrist between his fingers, pressed the cold disk of his stethoscope to her chest, but she clawed at him, too. Screamed at him to go away, let her die. He managed to slip a bitter pill beneath her tongue and tip a glass of water to her lips, the cold liquid quenching her raw, burning throat, spilling down the front of her nightgown.

Finally, she stopped screaming, stopping thrashing, and started to drift, her head fuzzy and thick. She closed her eyes and fell into a black, dreamless sleep.

When she awoke again, it was dark. Jim brought a tray with a steaming bowl of broth and cup of tea. He tried to coax a spoonful of broth into her mouth, but she pushed the spoon away and shoved the tray, spilling the broth, dumping the tea. He slipped another pill beneath her tongue and the blackness returned.

Her mother-in-law came and laid cold cloths on her forehead, but Jean swatted at her hands, threw the cloths across the room, yelled at her to leave. Jim gave her another pill and she gladly tumbled back into the abyss.

After five days, her fever broke. The pills stopped, the blackness lifted.

But, still, Jean couldn't get out of bed. She continued to sleep, through the daylight, through the night. She again dreamed of Sandy in the tub, of the little boy with the missing front teeth, and moldy bread.

She couldn't eat. Baby Larry toddled to the side of the bed and cried for her. She rolled away from him and put the pillow over her head.

More days passed.

She stared at the ceiling. She stared out the window at the driveway. Snow fell. She didn't speak. Sometimes she cried silently and then fell asleep with her cheek pressed against the cold, wet circle on her pillow.

Weeks passed.

February became March.

One morning Jim brought a tray of buttered toast, scrambled eggs and three slices of bacon. He set the tray down on the bed and kneeled next to her with his hands clasped beneath his chin as if he were about to pray. She stared at him, waiting for him to say something.

Instead, he began to weep. Hard, raking sobs that shook his entire body. Fat tears rolled down his ruddy cheeks and dripped from the tip of his nose onto the floor.

"Please eat," he cried. "I can't stand to see you like this. Me and little Larry need you."

She'd never seen her husband cry.

And so, finally, she ate. She ate the eggs first. She chewed and swallowed to make her husband happy. She ate the bacon.

He stroked her matted hair. "That's a good girl," he said.

She took a bite of toast.

"You gave me quite a scare," he said.

"I'm sorry," she said. Her voice was hoarse. She hadn't spoken in days.

He took her hand and laced his fingers through hers.

"Jean." He said her name carefully, as if testing out the sound and her reaction to it. "What happened to Sandy, it wasn't your fault."

She stopped chewing.

"Miscarriages are terrible and there was nothing you could've done. That doctor in Janesville said so." The fat tears started to roll again. "I know she was your friend and it must've been terrible what you saw in that motel, but there wasn't anything you could've done. You didn't know."

She dropped the toast.

Jean extracted her fingers from Jim's and rolled over onto her side. She couldn't bear to see her husband cry again or to hear those words one more time. *There wasn't anything you could've done.*

"I'm better now, Jim," she said in the most convincing tone she could muster so her husband would leave her alone. "I just need to rest. Can you please turn off the light?"

Jim sighed. He picked up the tray. He hesitated at the door.

"Tommy's downstairs," he said. "Can he come up for just a minute? He really wants to see you. He's been waiting for weeks."

She didn't answer and pulled the blanket over her shoulders.

She'd known Tommy would come. She'd known she would have to eventually face him, answer his questions.

"I suppose," she finally said. She sat up and slipped on her glasses.

Jim left, and a few moments later there was a soft knock at her bedroom door. She called him in.

Tommy entered. His eyes were red-rimmed and he had a few days growth of pale stubble on his face. He pulled a rocking chair up to the side of her bed and sat down.

"How are you?" he said.

"Okay," she answered.

He studied her face. "You look like you've lost some weight."

She didn't respond.

"I'm glad you're better," he said. "Doc Cleary said you were really sick. A fever that high can be dangerous."

She looked at the window.

Tommy picked up the skeleton key to Jean's sewing room from the nightstand and began to play with it.

"I can't believe she's gone," he said, his voice cracking.

Heavy, wet snowflakes were falling and melting against the glass pane.

"Did Jim tell you they buried her in Algoma?" Tommy asked. "Next to her grandparents. Her parents wouldn't allow me at the funeral."

She looked up at the ceiling. She didn't want to hear this.

"We were in love," he said.

She made no move, no expression.

"It started last summer," he continued. "It just kind of turned from friendship into sweethearts. But we kept it a secret from everyone because her parents are so strict." The words tumbled out of him, a confession.

The room grew dim from the clouds. The features of Tommy's face softened and became undefined.

He lifted his head and looked directly into Jean's eyes, the blue of his own bright and sharp with wetness. "Did you know?" he asked. "That she was pregnant?"

Jean shrank into the pillow, pinned down by his intense stare. She'd been asked this very question by the motel clerk, the men in the ambulance, the doctor in Janesville. Her answer was so practiced she no longer felt the lie.

"No." She shook her head, numbly, mechanically. "I had no idea until I found her that morning, after..."

Tommy's face cracked and he began to weep. "I loved her," he cried. "I really loved her. I would've married her no matter what. If she'd just told me."

Jean looked back at the widow and felt an acidic lump rise in her throat as if she might vomit. She thought of that moment in her basement, weeks ago, when Sandy had first confessed about the baby and the affair with Tommy, and her worries about whether or not Tommy would marry her out of obligation. And in that moment in her basement, even before Tommy confirmed it himself, Jean had known he'd marry Sandy for love.

And, more importantly, Jean could finally admit that what she had done during that trip to Chicago had been for herself, not for Sandy. There is no greater glory than love, her mother used to say, nor a greater punishment than jealousy.

Tommy wiped his eyes and raked his fingers through his hair.

"I'm sorry," he said. "Carrying on like this after what you've been through. I should probably let you get some rest."

He moved to the side of the bed and gathered her in his arms. "You're a good friend, Jean," he said. "I'm glad at least you were there with her."

He cradled the back of her head and pulled her face against his chest. She stiffened in his embrace at first, but then relaxed. She reached her arms up and wrapped them around his neck, her fingers brushing the soft hairs at his collar. That old, familiar longing deep in her gut took hold.

She had but one choice—to get on with the business of life.

She would atone for her sins. She would make it up to Tommy. She had a lifetime to try.

Jean released Tommy and opened her bedside table drawer. She removed the green velvet box.

"Here," she said, handing Sandy's pearls to him.

He hesitated. "She gave them to you."

"I know," she said, "but you should have something of hers."

He took the box and stroked the velvety top. "Thank you," he said after a moment. "These mean a lot to me."

He squeezed her shoulder and left the room.

The snow was falling heavier now and piling up on the windowsill.

Jean closed her eyes. Just the small act of giving Tommy the pearls made her feel like the crushing weight and grief that had rendered her crippled was starting to lighten.

Yes, she could start anew. She had been given a second chance.

Jean folded her hands beneath her chin and began to pray. Never again would she succumb to her jealousy and malice, the worms in her blood. Never again would she hurt herself or lie and deceive in the name of envy.

It's a difficult life to live so close to what you cannot have. Remember that, Jean Gillman.

She would prove Eunice wrong. She would accept her life for what it was.

She got out of bed and dressed in a clean pair of pants and a warm sweater. There were chores to do. Laundry to wash. Meals to cook. A baby to care for. The business of life.

Once dressed, she took the skeleton key from the bedside table. At the end of the hall, she locked the door to the sewing room Jim had made for her. Downstairs, she hung the key on a nail in a kitchen cabinet where they stored all the other anonymous, orphaned household keys.

She hadn't much use for it anymore.

CHAPTER 21

Labor Day, 1964

Jean picked the last mess of tomatoes from her garden, retying the plants to their wooden stakes and straightening the metal cages as she worked her way down a row. It had been her best tomato crop in years due to the Indian summer. She filled a gallon feed bucket to the rim with beefsteak, cherry, and Roma tomatoes, barely able to lug it to the porch. Rubbing a cramp from her hand, she watched, squinting through her old pair of glasses—she had yet to fix her good pair—as a stray orange tabby cat stalked the birds at her goldfinch feeder hanging from a post under the oak tree. The tom crouched back on his haunches, eyes fixed on the flittering birds above him, and prepared to pounce.

"Shoo!" Jean shouted, stamping her foot against the porch planks. "Scram or I'll swat you with the broom!" She picked a tomato out of the bucket and hurled it across the yard. The cat finally startled and scurried away to the barn.

Inside, Jean dumped the tomatoes into the sink. It was noon, already time to make lunch for the men in the fields as they had worked straight through the holiday weekend. The weeks spent chopping and hauling silage were some of the toughest of the year on the farm. Not only were the days long and demanding, but something inevitably went wrong—busted wagon axles, tractors stuck in muddy fields, broken chains and belts on the machinery.

She wearily went about fixing a dozen or more ham and

cheese sandwiches, bags of sliced vegetables, peanut butter cookies and a jug of ice water. She was exhausted after another poor night of sleep. It had been happening more and more since the Sunday dinner announcement a few weeks ago. Jean would awaken multiple times in a single night, jolted by some vague noise, a phantom thud or thump from nondescript places in the house, and she would immediately shake Jim awake. He would dutifully roll out of bed and stumble about in his jockey shorts to conduct a search with yawns and droopy eyelids, only to return shortly after finding nothing amiss. Eventually, she stopped waking him and simply lay in bed, wide-eyed and staring into the darkness, clutching the edges of the sheet drawn up to her chin, waiting for sleep to return or the next noise, whichever came first. This disruption, this carping disharmony she experienced all night, was breeding an unpleasant side effect of paranoia in Jean, to the point where she was even checking over her shoulder in daylight. For what, she didn't know.

Finished, Jean carried the food in a box, balanced on her hip like a baby, and draped the handle of the water jug over her arm. Outside, James sat on the porch rail looking bored, swinging his feet and sucking on a Popsicle.

"What are you doing?" he asked. His tongue was blood red and drip marks dotted the front of his shirt.

"Taking lunch out to the men." Jean readjusted the handle of the jug.

"Can I come? Dad said I could ride with him this afternoon."

"Yes, here. Take this," Jean said and handed him the jug. "Don't drop it."

Jean and James made their way around the barn to the bunker where the men had been putting up the last of the silage ten hours a day for almost a week. They stepped safely aside and waited as Jim rumbled by in a tractor pulling a silage wagon, rattling and banging over the rutted dirt roads, kicking up an enormous wall of dust. Jean coughed and clenched her eyes shut against the gritty cloud. Specks of dirt landed on James's popsicle and he tossed it into the weeds.

Jim circled on a tight turnabout, aligned with the grain auger, and dropped open the small conveyor door on the side of the wagon. He switched on the auger motor and revved up the tractor, sending clumps of the moist, chopped up corn and stalks tumbling from the wagon into the auger mouth, where it then traveled up the tube and poured out into a massive heap in the nearly full bunker. Tommy waited atop with a tractor and blade to spread out and pack down the silage. Once full, they would cover it with large black tarps weighed down by old tractor tires.

Jean waved at Jim, pointing to the box of food, and he gestured her over. She and James crossed the lane toward him and wrinkled their noses against the sour, pungent odor of silage juice that oozed from the dozens of cracks in the aged concrete wall panels, formed by the combination of acid and years of weather exposure. Jean had never minded the sweet scent of freshly chopped silage, pleasant in the same way as cut grass, but the stench of silage drainage was just awful. Almost as bad as hogs.

Jean picked her way through a scratchy patch of shattercane and cocklebur weeds to where Jim supervised the unloading wagon. James handed him the jug of ice water and plugged his fingers into his ears.

"Ham and cheese!" Jean yelled over the deafening machinery.

"Great!" Jim said. He gulped down several mouthfuls of water. "I'm starving!"

Jean nodded and handed him two sandwiches from the box. James wandered over to a patch of milkweeds and began picking the pods. He cracked one open and fingered the silky insides.

Jim cupped his hand around his mouth. "We're about

done."

"Good!" Jean shouted back. "You need to breed a heifer this afternoon before you start milking."

Tommy roared by the edge of the bunker above them on the John Deere 4020, too close to the edge on some passes. Jean would tell him to be more careful when he came down for lunch. Large black headphones covered his ears like winter earmuffs, so Jean caught his attention by waving her arms and pointing at the box of food. He gave her a smile and tipped his cap, and then disappeared once more when he raised the front blade and turned the tractor in the opposite direction.

Jean slapped a horsefly off her leg. "James wants to ride with you for a while," she said.

Jim gave her a thumbs up and stuffed the last bite of his sandwich into his mouth. Jean brushed a crumb from his mustache. He grinned and swiped an extra cookie. Up close, she could see spidery lines of dirt streaking his face. He removed his shirt and doused himself with a handful of cold water from the jug. In all the years she'd known him, he'd had mismatched body parts. His dark, permanently tanned face, neck and forearms were a stark contrast to the white skin of his chest and back, so defined it looked almost as if he were wearing a shirt when he really wasn't. But, after so many years, his body had become something of a familiar comfort to her.

When Jim realized Jean was staring at him, her expression soft, he paused to kiss her on the cheek. They exchanged a tender smile. He slipped back into his shirt and resituated his cap. As he reached for the rail to climb up into the tractor, a loud crackling sound erupted behind them. In the same second they both turned, the top half of a concrete wall panel on the bunker began to buckle with Tommy on the 4020 just inches away. He saw the failing section and instinctively cranked the wheel to steer away from it. Silage began to pour from the fissure, like water from a breached levee, and the tractor tilted ominously to one side.

Jean's free hand fluttered to her glasses, her farsighted vision compromised and undependable in the old pair, as if a mere adjustment of the spectacles on her nose would change the scene before her.

"Jesus Christ!" Jim screamed, shutting down the auger. "Tommy! Tommy!"

The entire wall crumbled and gave way, sending thousands of pounds of concrete and silage barreling to the ground.

Jean dropped the box of food on her feet. "Don't!" she cried, a singular word that came out like a hysterical laugh and scream.

Realizing what was happening, Tommy tried to gun the tractor but it stalled for a sickening second, and then slid backward before completely turning over on top of itself. Tommy's body, arms and legs flailing as if made of rubber, was instantly swallowed by the avalanche. His blue cap came to rest on top of a slab of fractured concrete.

It was over in a matter of seconds. Everything went still but for a few lines of silage trickling down the wreckage like a leaky pipe. The front tires of the tractor protruded straight up to the sky, still spinning. Jim clamored to the top of the debris pile, screaming Tommy's name, clawing concrete boulders out of his way.

Jean's arms dropped to her sides and she stood motionless, disbelieving. James stood oblivious in the milkweed patch, white feathery seeds floating softly about him like snow.

CHAPTER 22

September, 1964

Jean stood at her kitchen sink, arms crossed tightly over her chest, as she waited for the basin to fill with hot water.

Tommy was dead.

Unthinkable.

She stared vacantly out the window, watching Jim help Liz escort the last of the reception guests off the porch to their cars. Liz appeared frail and small in her loose black dress, as if a light breeze could send her rolling down the driveway.

Jean kicked off her black pumps and tenderly poked at a blister just under her nylons on the back of her ankle. She rubbed the bottom of her other foot and felt a gap in the material of her hose—a run that stretched from the seam at her toes up to the middle of her calf. She'd probably walked around with it all day. She hiked up her dress and stripped off the nylons, stuffing them into the trash in a wadded-up ball.

Tommy's death had rocked the residents of Redwood County. Wives had tied up phone lines for the past three days as dinners made it to the table late and babies fussed, neglected in their playpens. *Joyce Culp told me they shocked him three times at the hospital and almost got a heartbeat. If they'd gotten him out just a minute or two sooner, they could've saved him, just a minute or two.* County roads found trucks stopped in pairs at intersections, farmers deep in conversation window to window. *I damn near died when I rolled one down a crick bank back in '58.*

Parishioners filled the churches of Chickering the Sunday following the accident and the Methodist Women's Group took up a collection for Liz and the baby, managing to raise $325 in a matter of hours. The day of the funeral, many businesses closed their doors for the morning and a city police officer was posted to help manage parking at the Methodist church.

A woman on Liz's porch, the last guest to leave, hugged her goodbye. Jim trudged across the yards with a small box tucked under his arm. He slipped into the house and sat down at the table, resting the box on his knees. He removed a small container of chewing tobacco from his front jacket pocket and pinched a dip between his bottom lip and gum. Jean snapped on a pair of yellow latex gloves and dunked a tray of dirty silverware, stacks of glasses and cake plates into the soapy water.

"Everyone gone?" she asked.

"Yep." He loosened the knot in his tie and slipped it from around his neck. "Larry's doing chores. Mother just went home." He rubbed the gray stubble already shadowing his jaw.

"It was a really nice turnout," Jean said. "And beautiful weather." Her voice had sounded practiced all day. The glasses gently clinked together in the dishwater as she wiped them out with a dishrag.

"Poor Liz," Jim said. "All alone and a baby on the way." He spat into an empty coffee mug. "She's already talking about moving back to Madison."

"Did she say anything about her parents coming to help her?"

Jim shook his head.

Jean gestured to the box still resting in Jim's lap. "What's that?"

Jim looked down as if noticing it for the first time. "Oh. Just a few things Liz gave me. Thought I'd like to have." He opened the flaps and pulled out a hunting knife, several cases of shotgun shells, a brass money clip and a dozen or so Indian arrowheads in perfect condition. He lined them up one at a time on the table. Lastly, he removed Tommy's baseball hat, his beloved Cubs cap, and gently set it in the center of the table.

He blew his nose into a handkerchief from his front pocket and stood. "Time to milk," he said, his voice hoarse. He gave her arm a single pat and kissed her cheek before going upstairs to change his clothes.

Jean slowly turned to look at the cap on the table, the once bright material now faded. She could hardly remember life before the Krenshaws and Tommy, before he was across the drive, just an arm's length away. Dizzy, Jean swayed and was forced to balance herself against the cabinet. She pressed a dishtowel to her mouth and finally allowed herself to weep. Hard sobs she'd been holding in for days wracked her body like waves from a storm battering against rocks.

She squeezed a glass in her hand tighter and tighter, fighting to catch her breath, until the glass exploded inside the pressure of her fist. She cried out and looked down with surprise at the broken pieces now floating in the soapy water. She stripped off the yellow glove to examine the skin. No cut.

A current of rage surged through her. Jean grabbed a floating piece of the broken glass and drove it deep into her palm. She gasped at the shock of it—the pain, the ferocity, the gravity of the injury, and the overwhelming relief.

"I'm going out," Jim said, startling her.

"Oh, okay." She grabbed the dishtowel and held it to her now bleeding palm.

"The demo crew is coming next Monday, so we need to start getting the silage moved out first thing tomorrow morning. Jean? Are you listening?"

"What? Oh, yes, the bunker. I heard you." She tucked her hand close to her waist.

"I'll be glad to get that god damn thing torn down." Jim shoved his feet into a pair of rubber work boots and clomped across the porch. A breeze caught and slammed the screen door behind him and Jean flinched at the sound.

Carefully, she pulled the towel away and examined the wound. It was far deeper than she'd intended, or than she'd ever inflicted before, and probably needed stitches. The mere wiggling of her fingers sent hot flashes of pain searing through her entire hand.

Blood ran down her wrist and dripped into the dishwater. She took a deep breath and reapplied the towel. There would be no hiding it. She would have to make up a story. Some silly household injury. An accidental stab with a butcher knife while she was trying to cut something tough. A frozen chicken breast. Yes. That would do.

With her good hand, she picked the broken pieces of glass out of the sink and dropped them into the garbage can. She held up the large shard she'd cut herself with and looked through it like a kaleidoscope, watching everything warp and change around her.

After several seconds, she dropped the shard into the trash and continued cleaning out the sink.

CHAPTER 23

Winter, 1965

The last warm days of autumn sunshine felt like a cruel contrast to the loss of Tommy. The children went back to school and every day for a week Jean forgot to send milk money. Halloween passed, then Thanksgiving. The unseasonably nice weather lingered. When the first snow finally fell in early December, Jean was unprepared and hadn't yet brought the children's winter clothes and snow boots down from the attic, so they were forced to wear double layers of shirts and their sneakers to school instead.

She stopped making her potato salad.

Liz's belly grew bigger. At Christmas, she announced she'd found an apartment in Madison near the university and would move back soon, before the baby was born. She was round and puffy, and carrying high. Jean thought she looked like she was having a girl.

One early January morning, Jean was in the barn working with a laboring cow. The heifer had already been laboring for many hours the day and night before and was now in trouble. She thrashed her legs against the wooden slats of the narrow pen, kicking up straw soiled with long strings of bloody tissue and membrane. Her black eyes watered with bits of dirt stuck to the end of her wet nose, and two legs protruded from her back end like a pair of chopsticks. First calves were often difficult and needed assistance, but this one was breech and taking too long. And Jean always hated pulling breech calves.

Tommy had always delivered them.

She slipped on a plastic glove almost up to her shoulder and removed a metal OB chain from a nail on the wall. The heifer bleated a hoarse cry as Jean inserted her gloved hand up to her elbow to confirm the calf's backward position. She then looped the middle section of the chain around the two exposed legs, grasped the ends and wrapped them around her hands and wrists. She pulled slowly, red-faced and grimacing from the effort as her right foot slid on the dirt floor, the left braced against the cow's back hip for stability. The heifer bawled, her mouth wide and long salmon pink tongue rigid. The calf's body finally gave way and slipped out of its mother with the placenta in a bloody, slimy puddle.

Jean let go of the chain and leaned against the stall slats and wiped a layer of cold sweat from her brow. The large newborn, a bull, lay motionless on the ground. She immediately suctioned the mucous out of his nose and mouth with a rubber bulb syringe. She then grabbed a small handful of clean straw and stuck it up the calf's nose, trying to force him to sneeze or snort and hopefully draw his first breath, but he didn't respond. She wiped him down with a clean calving blanket in an attempt to dry and warm him, but his head continually lolled around loose and uncontrolled, his eyes fixed. He was clearly stillborn.

Jean covered the dead calf with the blanket and turned her attention to the ailing heifer. She slapped the cow's ass end and the heifer struggled up into a wobbly gait on weak hind legs, and she managed to stay upright for only a few minutes before collapsing onto her knees. Jean fought again to get her up—slapping, pushing, shouting and pulling her with a neck harness, but the heifer wouldn't budge. After spotting a telltale kink in the cow's neck, she suspected the animal had developed Milk Fever, a potentially fatal condition that could only be treated with intravenous salt and calcium, so Jean telephoned old Doc Vinton from the parlor. Mrs. Vinton said he was already on another call at another farm and would make it over to their place as soon as he could. Jean hung up the phone and walked to the barn door. She pushed it open, revealing a full view of the farm gently sloping away to the clear north horizon. To the east, the windows of Tommy's house were still dark at this hour.

Except, it wasn't Tommy's house anymore.

The realization that he was gone still knocked the wind out of her sometimes.

Liz had been slowly packing the farm house for months—sorting, organizing, boxing up items, giving items away—but her growing belly made faster progress than her packing. She was now a mere seven weeks away from giving birth and still not ready to move.

Privately, Jean was desperate for her to leave. She couldn't articulate why, but Liz's lingering presence felt like a noose around Jean's neck with which she could hang herself at any moment. The sooner Liz was gone, the better for everyone.

Jean turned away from the house and its dark, empty windows. From the corner of her eye, she spotted a pale blue button-up shirt hanging from a nail. She lifted it.

Tommy's shirt, she recognized. The one he'd been wearing the day the cows got out, when he'd put his arm around her and she'd pressed her nose to that small pool above his collarbone. Soap and faint musk.

She pushed her fingertips into the corners of her eyes, painfully, like a cork in a bottle, to prevent the spring of tears. She inhaled deep, steady breaths and counted to ten, twenty. If she started, if she gave in every time, she might never stop. There was no taking to her bed as she'd done after Sandy died. This grief she had no choice but to keep private.

Thirty. Forty. The burning in the back of her throat and behind her eyes finally subsided.

Jean carefully folded the shirt and tucked it into her coat

pocket. She pulled her knit stocking cap further down over her ears and buried her cold hands into a pair of wool gloves. Exhausted, she sat down on the ground next to the ailing heifer and dozed off.

When she awoke, groggy and stiff, she checked her wristwatch and was surprised to see that nearly an hour and a half had passed since she'd called Doc Vinton. She hurried back to the stall and immediately saw that the heifer had laid out flat onto her side. Jean flung off her gloves and dropped to her knees. The cow's eyes had widely dilated and her muzzle was dry. Her breaths were quick and shallow. Jean ran her hands along the bony ridges of the cow's head, over her cold, drooping ears, her bloated belly, and then down her equally cold legs. All signs of imminent death, Jean knew.

She frantically tied the harness around the cow's head and neck once more and attempted to pull her up to her feet, but there was no muscle response. She covered her with the last of the warming blankets and rolled every empty gunnysack she could find and stuffed them beneath the underside of the cow in an effort to prop her up, but it was too late. The heifer took a dozen final shallow gasps of air and died.

Jean collapsed hard on the straw-covered ground. She'd never lost both a heifer and calf at the same time before. She dropped her chin to her chest and closed her eyes. Death followed her everywhere, it seemed.

She began to shiver and jammed her hands into her pockets. Her clenched fist pushed against the folded fabric of Tommy's shirt, and the old memory of Eunice's words filled her head, along with the piercing screams of the white owls. She clamped her hands over her ears.

"Jean?"

Jean dropped her arms and stood, shaking and unsteady.

Doc Vinton stood in the doorway of the barn, staring at her. She straightened her cap.

"I...the heifer and calf didn't make it," she said.

He stepped through the doorway and looked into the stall. "I'm sorry," he said. "I got here as soon as I could."

Jean covered her mouth with her hand and thought for a moment she was going to scream, uncork the bottle.

"I couldn't save them," she finally said.

CHAPTER 24

February 10, 1965

Jean bolted upright in bed from a sound sleep. One of the boys had called out for her. She blinked hard several times, listening. No, the telephone on the hall table had rung, she realized. A single shrill peal, and then silence. Yes, it had been the telephone. Not one of the phantom noises that had been haunting her for months. She waited, staring through the darkness at the ceiling. She groped around the bedside table for her glasses, bumping photo frames and a reading lamp before locating them. Alert, she noticed the steady sound of icy rain pattering against the roof. The clock read just after midnight. She glanced at Jim sleeping next to her, blissfully unbothered without his new hearing aids.

Unsettled, Jean rose and padded into the hallway, her feet growing cold on the chilly floorboards. She paused, listening to the quiet house once more. She lifted the telephone receiver, heard the dial tone, and hung it back up.

She poked her head into the younger boys' bedroom and switched off the dangling naked bulb in the closet with a sigh—William was always leaving lights on around the house and Jean was forever trailing behind, shutting them off with a tired lecture on wasting electricity. She went downstairs and methodically moved around the kitchen. She checked the oven, the burners on the stove, even her iron hanging on a hook in the broom closet, but everything was as it should be. She filled a glass of water from the tap and plucked a gingersnap from the cookie jar. As she returned to her bedroom, the telephone rang again and she yelped with a start. She snatched up the receiver before the second ring and coughed to clear her throat.

"Hello?"

There was a pause and then a rustling sound, as if someone had dropped the phone and was fumbling to pick it up.

"Hello?" The female voice on the other end answered muffled and distant. "Jean?"

"Liz?"

Liz mumbled something else inaudible.

"What? Say that again." Jean pressed her finger over her other ear, as if there were a racket in the background instead of a sleeping house.

"Jean, I'm sick. My head...I need...I need you to come over."

"Is it the baby?"

"No...I don't know," Liz mumbled. "I'm really sick."

"I'll be right there," Jean said. She replaced the phone on the cradle, her heartbeat slowing.

She pulled the clothes she'd been wearing earlier in the day from the hamper and shed her warm flannel nightdress quickly, shivering in the chilly air. She shook Jim awake to tell him where she was going. He mumbled a response and quickly went back to sleep.

In the mudroom, she slipped into a pair of boots and her green knitted cardigan. As she crossed the yards, she huddled deeper into her sweater and leaned into the icy, driving rain, wishing she'd worn a heavy coat.

Jean entered the darkened house without knocking and Dixie began to bark. Jean quickly shushed her.

"Liz?" she called, easily moving through the mudroom identical to her own. Her stomach tightened for a moment as she took a deep breath. The house smelled of what she always thought of as Tommy—fresh soap and musk. She switched on a small light over the kitchen sink and squinted. The house was a mess with scattered boxes, dirty dishes and stacks of newspapers.

"Liz?" Jean called again. A small cough came from the living room. She followed the sound and turned on a lamp next to the sofa. Liz lay huddled under several layers of blankets, shielding her eyes against the light.

"Turn it off." She waved her hand, drawing into a tight ball, like a snail curling up into its shell. "My head..." she moaned. Her hair was pulled back into a crooked ponytail with strands falling loose around her puffy red face. She wore a loose maternity shift and, oddly, the pearls around her neck.

A bowl of cold oatmeal and plates of uneaten toast littered the floor alongside a mop bucket within arm's reach of the couch. Jean barely glanced at the smelly contents inside as she nudged it away with her foot.

"What's wrong? Are you in labor?" Jean asked.

Liz shook her head. "No," she grunted, painfully shifting to her opposite side. "I'm just sick."

Jean pressed the back of her hand against Liz's forehead and said, "Like the flu?" When did you start feeling like this?" Liz's skin was warm, bordering on hot. She moaned and her eyelids fluttered.

"Liz," Jean raised her voice. "Liz, how long have you been feeling bad?"

"A few days," she mumbled. "Sunday or Saturday."

"Where is your thermometer?"

Liz licked her dry lips. "Medicine cabinet."

Jean walked upstairs to the bathroom, Dixie following her every step, and searched several shelves before locating the glass thermometer in a blue plastic container. She ran a washcloth under cold tap water and returned to the living room. She laid the cloth over Liz's forehead and gave the thermometer a few hard shakes before slipping it under Liz's tongue. She kept time on her wristwatch.

After several minutes, she removed the thermometer from Liz's mouth.

"Let's see," she said, holding it up to the light to read the miniscule red line and numbers. "Ninety-nine point eight." She shook the mercury down a second time and planted her hands on her hips. "When's the last time you ate something?"

Liz clenched her eyes shut and made a face, pressing her hands to the crest of her belly. "No food," she said.

"You at least need to drink something. You're probably getting dehydrated. Have you had any diarrhea?"

Liz made a slight move to shake her head. "Just throwing up."

Jean went to the kitchen and heated a kettle of water on the stove for some tea. She returned with a steaming mug and a small plate of semi-stale soda crackers she found in the cabinet.

"Try a sip of this." She helped Liz into a sitting position.

"It's hot!" Liz recoiled.

"It's not bad. I tested it."

"I don't want it!"

"Liz, you need to get some fluids in you. Now just try one sip." Jean coaxed her to the mug once more.

Liz finally relented and took several drinks of the tea and even a few bites of cracker, and then sagged back into the pillow, exhausted from the small effort. "So sleepy..." she murmured and closed her eyes.

Jean let her rest. She rinsed out the bucket, washed the few dirty dishes and freshened the washcloth on Liz's forehead. She heard the milk truck rumble by the house to the stanchion barn to empty the tank for the next day's milking. It was almost one in the morning. She thought about calling Jim to tell him she'd probably be here all night and would need to take Liz in to the doctor first thing in the morning, but thought better of it. He'd never hear the phone.

Eventually, Jean dozed off in a chair and awoke around two-thirty to the sound of Liz vomiting, partly on herself and partly into the bucket.

"Oh, God!" Liz cried and fell back against the pillow. "My

head!"

Jean's heart did a small skip in her chest when she saw Liz's face, her cheeks so puffy that her eyes had nearly swollen shut.

"Maybe a cool bath would make you feel better," she said, her voice now tinged with worried uncertainty.

She managed to drag Liz, protesting every step of the way, upstairs to the bathroom where she filled the tub with cool water. When she gently stripped off Liz's soiled shift, she was troubled to see how swollen her legs were. Her olive skin was deeply lined with the impressions of her clothing seams, like a stitched-together rag doll, and Jean's fingers left dimples in Liz's calves. Liz's body—that taut, smooth canvas Jean had spied through the window—was now unrecognizable.

Liz lowered into the tub and her teeth began to chatter. "I'm so sick," she cried. "I...I want Tommy." She looked around the room with a drunken, half-lidded expression. "I, I have to get to the store. I need new oils. I'm painting a picture for him."

"Hush, now," Jean said. She dabbed Liz's runny nose and wiped the vomit from the ends of her hair with the washcloth. She unhooked the clasp of the pearls at the back of Liz's neck and slipped the necklace into the pocket of her cardigan so it wouldn't get wet. Once finished, Jean hoisted Liz from the tub and patted her dry, like a mother would a toddler.

In the bedroom, she propped Liz on the side of the bed while she searched for some clean clothes.

"Where are your undergarments?" she asked, opening and closing several drawers of the bureau.

"I need new paints," Liz murmured. She clutched the corners of the damp towel together as her eyelids drooped.

"Liz, where do you keep your undergarments? Your nightgowns?" Jean waited for an answer but Liz only covered her eyes against the light on the nightstand. Jean finally located a long flannel gown and a pair of thick socks in the bureau, but gave up on the underwear. When she unwrapped the towel and tried to lift Liz's arms over her head, Liz winced and cried out in pain.

"What, did that hurt?" Jean asked, standing back in alarm.

"My side...don't." Liz dug her fingers beneath her right ribs.

"Your side hurts?" Jean's voice raised in alarm. "How long has it been like this?"

Liz mumbled and waved her hand.

"Liz, how long?"

"This morning." Her eyes closed and she slowly sank back onto the bed. "I'll go to the store when, when the bread is done and...and..."

Jean pushed her glasses up the sweaty bridge of her nose as a sudden knot of fear twisted in her stomach. This wasn't the flu. There'd been a pregnant woman in town years ago—Jean could no longer recall her name—who'd fallen terribly ill shortly before her baby was due. Her blood pressure had gotten too high and, Jean remembered Alma Dawson telling her in great detail, the woman had suffered terrible pains under her ribs and those awful, swollen legs. By the time her husband had gotten her to the hospital in Janesville, she'd slipped into a coma and died two days later, along with the baby.

Jean hurriedly gathered the bucket and a pillow. "I need to get you to a hospital," she said. "Why on earth didn't you call Dr. Cleary when you started having problems?"

"I'm painting my Tommy a picture. Why isn't he home yet?" Liz mumbled. "It's a picture of our baby. I know it's a girl. Frances Elizabeth. Isn't that pretty? Tommy wants to call her Frannie."

"Mmm-hmm. That's lovely," Jean said distractedly. She lifted the telephone receiver on top of the bureau, trying to remember Dr. Cleary's home telephone number.

"My Tommy. I love him so much." Liz's voice suddenly became clear and loud. "You love my Tommy so much, too."

"What?" Jean knitted her brow, her finger poised over the dial.

Liz laughed with a snort. "I *said*, you love Tommy, too."

Jean turned, a disconcerted, half-twist with the phone cradled between her ear and shoulder. "What are you talking about? Of course I loved him. He was family."

"No," Liz said sharply. "Not like family. *In love* with him."

Jean's hand fell to her side. The words, their physical shapes and forms nearly visible to the naked eye, remained suspended in the soupy air between the women, floating free and dangerous.

Liz pushed a tangled lock of hair from her face. "He knew, too," she said. "He told me."

Jean took a step backward and bumped into the dresser. The noise of her own blood pumping filled her ears with a deafening roar, like the sound of water thundering over a waterfall. For a brief, insane moment, she saw herself lurch across the room—her graceless, gangly body for once lithe and quick—and wrap her hands around Liz's throat.

"I don't know what you're talking about," she whispered. She could hear the phone beeping. It had been off the hook for too long.

Liz pushed herself up to a sitting position. Her eyes grew wide and clear. "He told me before we got married," she said, her voice suddenly strong. "And we talk about it sometimes. How you watch him. How you've always watched him." She wriggled her fingers in the air. "Spy on him from your windows."

Jean pressed her clenched knuckles to the center of her brow, feeling faint. Dixie wandered into the room and sat at Jean's feet, patiently waiting for a scratch behind her ears. Jean stared down at the dog, her vision blurring with tears.

Liz pointed at Jean. "He told me he always knew how you felt about him, and he tried to just be your friend. He felt sorry for you." She paused and narrowed her eyes. "No. He felt sorry for *Jim*."

Jean slumped against the bureau and pressed the phone to her mouth until the hard plastic bit into the thin flesh of her bottom lip and she tasted blood.

Liz's lips slowly curled into a smile. "He called it the good divide," she said.

"What?" Tears were now running down Jean's cheeks.

"...the driveway." She coughed and wiped her nose with the heel of her hand. Her eyes were becoming unfocused again, her head starting to loll from side to side. "Tommy says to me all the time. He says the driveway is the only good divide between the houses." Her words slurred now.

Jean turned away and let the receiver fall from her hand. "You don't need to be cruel," she said, her voice breaking.

She laid her forehead against the smooth wood of the bureau, inhaling jagged breaths. Her body began to tremble, sway unsteadily. All those years, she'd thought she had hidden her feelings so well. She thought that Tommy had truly cared about her and appreciated her good efforts, when all along he'd made fun of her. *Pitied* her.

She saw her life as if viewing it for the first time. The hard, bright blind spot in her vision was gone, revealing at last an unfiltered picture of the landscape in which she lived, made up of compromised colors and painted by the hand of a fool.

Jean rooted around the deep pocket of her cardigan for a tissue, tangling the necklace with a hard object. Larry's pocketknife, she realized, forgotten in her sweater and thought lost since she'd confiscated it long ago at the Sunday dinner. She extracted it and examined the beautiful pearl handle. She slowly opened the blade and looked at her reflection in the shiny metal, ran her finger along the sharp edge. *He called it the good divide*. She pushed up the sleeve of her sweater and held the blade to a ropey blue vein on the inside of her wrist. *He felt sorry for you.*

Liz gasped and clutched her ribs through a sharp pain. She leaned over the side of the bed and dry heaved into the bucket, and then fell back against the pillow. Her eyelids fluttered and her entire body tensed, freezing into a queer, unnatural position.

Jean watched from over her shoulder, but did not move to help, the knife still pressed to her wrist. It was as if she had vacated her body and left her flesh standing as its own entity next to her. She became vaguely aware of subtle noises around her, singling themselves out one at a time. Sleet pattering against the roof. A rattling windowpane. Dixie's contented tail swishing and thumping against the floor. Outside, the distant bleat of a hungry calf.

All that time, he'd known how she felt about him. All that time and, still, he'd continued to tease, flirt, confide, eat her food, ask for favors with winks and smiles, knowing she'd oblige, that she'd never say no.

Liz lay motionless in the bed, her eyelids fixed open like crescent moons. A small line of saliva trickled out of the corner of her bluish lips. The mound of her belly, Tommy's baby, barely rose and fell with her shallow, labored breaths, until her belly stopped moving altogether.

Jean thought about Jim, asleep in their bed, and saw for the first time that it was his oblivious, unquestioning nature that had been the true compass of their marriage, keeping it on course and in smooth waters, not her honest or faithful nature as a wife.

She thought about her children, asleep in their beds, so innocent and trusting of everyone and everything around them.

And she thought about Eunice and that day at the picnic, how her warning for Jean had come true. Perhaps there was a curse on the houses. Perhaps she was the curse. Perhaps there was only one way to break it. For herself, for Jim, for her children.

Jean closed her eyes and allowed the thought to linger and take root. Her pounding heartbeat subsided, her breathing grew calm.

She reached out, watching the movement of her own arm

with an almost curious expression, and laid the receiver back onto its cradle. The angry beeping silenced.

She slipped the knife back into the pocket of her cardigan with the pearls.

She switched off the lamp next to the bed.

She walked out of the bedroom and down the stairs on stiff legs, taking her time to push each large button of her cardigan through the eyelets. She turned off the remaining lights in the living room and left, closing the door behind her.

Outside, Jean stood on the porch for a moment and took a deep, cold breath. She descended the stairs and walked around the house and across the yard. The driving sleet felt sharp against her face and quickly soaked through her sweater and pants. She continued walking, slow and unhurried, behind the barn to the slab of pavement where she'd once smashed her beloved crystal bowl. There, she sat down.

The road to hell is paved with good intentions, her mother once said. But there had been no good intentions, Jean knew. Her road had been paved with humiliation, lies, and death. And Tommy had given her road a name.

She removed the pearls from her pocket and held them in the palm of her hand for a moment. She drew the necklace around her neck and fastened the clasp, running her fingers along each fine smooth pearl.

She rolled up both sleeves of her cardigan to her elbows, and opened Larry's knife. She held the blade to the skin of one wrist, ready. She had cut hundreds of times before and this time would be no different.

Relief, always relief, was the goal.

MISTRESSES

I awake to a hand slapping the other side of my wall. It startles me and I blink stupidly a few times at the plaster, my eyes trying to adjust to the darkness. I'm in no hurry to get out of bed.

I dress and shuffle about the chilly house, making just enough noise to let her know I am up and out of bed, doing all the things I do for her each morning without fail. Brew the coffee. Put her oatmeal on the stove to cook. Organize her half-dozen pills. Set out her clothes.

I enter Liz's bedroom, which smells faintly of urine most of the time, just as she is about to take an angry, impatient swing at the nightstand with her good hand because I've taken too long to get up and get going.

I part the curtains and a pale shaft of early light stretches across the bed, over the two flabby lumps of her legs. I look out the window. Each year I approach this day with caution, like tip-toeing around a sleeping junkyard dog.

Today is February 28th, Frances's birthday. She is twenty years old.

It's been twenty years ago today, since that disastrous, life-changing night.

I point to the smudged sky. "Looks like snow again," I say. "The weatherman said forty-two percent chance this afternoon."

Liz stares at me. She is silent and motionless but her eyes follow my every move. It used to unnerve me, but now, after all this time, I am used to it.

"Pink or lavender?" I hold up two dressing gowns from

the bureau, one in each hand, but she only stares. I know she can't answer, unable to speak since the stroke, but I would rather hear my own ridiculous voice than the silence.

"Right." I nod. "Pink, it is."

I peel the covers back and lift her nightdress up to her waist. "And dry this morning," I say.

I remove the bunched up cloth diaper and slide a bedpan beneath her hips. I pause to examine the start of a bedsore in the folds of wrinkled skin on the side of her right buttocks. I find a tube of ointment in the nightstand and squeeze a dollop onto my fingertip. Just as the drop-in nurse showed me, I gently dab it onto the sore and cover it with a bandage, massaging the area to get some circulation going again. I remove the bedpan when she's done and dump it in the toilet. I finish dressing her.

"Well," I sigh. "I've got to make a pie today for the church fundraiser on Saturday. Did I tell you the church needs a new roof? It leaked during that heavy rain last October and ruined two rows of choir chairs and hymnals."

Liz exhales loudly through her nose, shifting her gaze away.

"Oh, I guess I probably told you that already." I straighten and push my glasses up the bridge of my nose. I know I repeat myself occasionally. But sometimes it is on purpose because I have nothing new to say.

I align her wheelchair with the side of the bed, lock the wheels, and help her to a sitting position with my hands under her armpits.

"On three," I say and heave her into the chair after a slow count. It is an awkward system and I have dropped her on more than one occasion, but it is the best I can do.

"There," I pant. I have to sit on the side of the bed to catch my breath and rub an aching spot in the middle of my lower back. I clumsily braid and pin her long hair, greasy between my fingers, into a bun at the back of her head. It needs a good wash but the drop-in nurse doesn't come to give her a bath until tomorrow. I cannot do the baths alone anymore because of my arthritis.

I push her into the kitchen, the rubber wheels squealing against the linoleum, and lock the brakes at the table. I spoon up small bites of the oatmeal and she opens and closes her lips slowly for each mouthful, the effort of the controlled movements sending her neck muscles into a mild fit of tremors. The oatmeal smears across her mouth.

The telephone rings and I check the time. Too early for a birthday phone call from Frances, so it must be Larry, calling with his daily check-in that I can time by the clock. It's the mid-break of the early milking, when he stops to eat the breakfast his wife, Laura, has brought out to him before she puts their kids on the bus for school. Yes, I am familiar with that routine.

I take the bowl with me to answer the phone. "Hello, Larry," I say. They are always quick, efficient conversations: who is driving me to church and who is staying with Liz on Sunday, the toilet is leaking again, no, I do not want Suzanne, Will's wife, to bring me leftover roast today. I don't tell him that her roasts are too dry.

When I hang up and turn back to Liz, she has dozed off and her head is drooping forward. Dried bits of oatmeal are stuck to her chin. From this angle, the top of her head is illuminated by the harsh overhead light and I can see the bulging line of the shunt through her thin skin and hair, running down the side of her head, behind her ear and down her neck, like a drain from a sink.

I put aside the unfinished oatmeal and use the chance to scrub my kitchen floor. Old habits die hard, my mother used to say.

Once finished, I venture outside for the mail. Many days it is the only time I get out of the house. I no longer have a vegetable garden or flowerbeds or birdfeeders. Just a post under the front tree where Will nails ears of corn for the squirrels whenever he remembers. Mindful of the icy ground,

I walk slowly to the rusty mailbox, the white painted letters of KRENSHAW nearly worn off since the days when Bonnie lived here.

I miss my old mailbox. I miss my garden, and flowerbeds, and birdfeeders. I my old house on the main farm, with its comforting twin just across the driveway.

I pry open the squeaky door and find the newspaper and two envelopes, one actually addressed to Crystal (the new mailman is so careless) but the other is in familiar female handwriting. My pace back to the house quickens with excitement.

"It's a letter from Frances!" I announce as soon as I enter, waving the envelope above my head.

Liz's eyes snap open and when she lifts her head, the tremors dissipate. I tear open the seal and find a snapshot of Frances, posing behind a podium wearing a smart blue dress and her Alice in Dairyland sash and gold and platinum tiara. I unfold the single-page letter containing a few small paragraphs and begin to read aloud.

"Dear Aunt Jean—"

My dentures slip and I stop to press them back to the roof of my mouth with my thumb, start again:

February 26th, 1987

Dear Aunt Jean,

What a month I've had! It feels like I've been on the road for three weeks straight. As soon as I got back from the World Ag Expo in California (and CA was so much fun!), I had to turn right around and head to Green Bay for a dairyman's conference. I was hoping to make it home for my birthday, but tomorrow I'm off to Milwaukee for a meet-and-

greet thing and then another farm show in Eau Claire in early March. I hope to get back to the farm for Mother's Day weekend when I have a small break in my schedule. Thank you for the knit scarf and box of birthday cookies. They're delicious, as always. I can't believe I'm 20. I feel so old!

More exciting news! They're sending me to Canada in April for the Canadian Dairy Expo! I'm so excited I can hardly stand it! My first time out of the country.

Anyway, I have to run. You'll probably get this before the 28th, so I'll try to call on my birthday after I get to Milwaukee and check into my hotel. James is taking me out for dinner when he gets off work at the firm.

Please kiss Mom for me.

All my love,
Frances

When I finish, I look at Liz but cannot read her face. Her expression remains unchanged while she stares out the window. She has suffered memory loss from so many seizures, and it is hard to tell what she does or does not understand. I tack the letter and picture to a small bulletin board next to the phone that is crowded with school photos of my grandchildren and old snapshots chronicling Frances's childhood. Frances in a diaper taking her first step on chubby legs. Pigtailed Frances peddling around the yard on a bicycle. First day of kindergarten. First formal dance in a peach satin dress. High school graduation in a cap and gown. She looks so much like her father it takes my breath away.

Tommy's daughter. Liz's daughter.

And, by inheritance, my daughter.

I can still hear her voice when she would get home from school and burst through the door each day. *Aunt Jeeean! It's meee!* Like the sweet whistle of a teakettle.

It is already late morning. I can never understand where the time goes. Despite so little to do with my days anymore, they still manage to slip through my fingers, like trying to get a firm grip on a handful of water. I finish my pie to get it in the oven before I will have to start on lunch. I then decide to make a chocolate cake—Frances's favorite—to mark her birthday.

As I start to mix ingredients for the cake, I think that I will stop at the cemetery on my way home from the church tomorrow and put flowers on Jim's grave. I think about the last evening I spent with Jim in this very room, two years ago now. We had already retired from the dairy farm and moved with Liz into Bonnie's old house by that point. I had made a pot of steaming beef stew with homemade bread, and Jim and I had eaten seconds, plus melting scoops of ice cream for dessert. Afterwards, we'd both retired to our recliners in front of the six o'clock news, and Jim had quickly dozed off. Sitting in my chair next to him, a sewing project on my lap, I remember thinking how nice it was that all I had to do was stretch my arm out and there he would be. How I had taken it for granted he would always be there. Because little did I know, he had a bad heart with clogged arteries, just like his grandmother Beatrice. It was fast and painless. I didn't even know he'd gone until I tried to wake him to go to bed.

The boys were already grown and married and running the farm by then and Frances was in college, so after Jim died, it was just me and Liz. Alone, the remaining years of our lives unspooling before us like a long ribbon of empty highway.

We are no longer interesting gossip like we once were.

Bigger stories eventually upstaged all the Krenshaw family dramas from twenty and thirty years ago. In '71, Alma and Howard Dawson were audited by the IRS and found to owe thousands in unpaid taxes, not to mention the discovery of Howard's little girlfriend in Janesville, who had been well-kept and living high on the hog for over a decade. Alma, now divorced, lives with Beverly in Wautoma, and Howard left the country with the girlfriend, never to be seen again. The Chickering Elementary School was burned to the ground in '79 by arsonists and a three-year investigation never did turn up any guilty parties. The Krenshaws had escaped the worst of the farm crisis of the mid-80's, only to see neighboring small, family-owned dairies disappearing, now getting run off by corporate operations ten times bigger. But that's more Larry's and William's worry than mine anymore. Yes, the Krenshaws are old news.

Sometimes, when I bump into old friends and neighbors in town, they'll hug me and tell me how much they miss the old days when Jim, Tommy and I used to throw the grandest Fourth of July parties. They tell me how much those Krenshaw boys are still missed. They tell me I'm a saint for caring for my widowed, invalid sister-in-law all these years and for raising her daughter as my own. Like the doctors at the hospital in Janesville said—once Frances had been safely delivered by C-section—Liz and the baby surely would've died from the preeclampsia, had it not been for me.

They tell me I'm a saint, and it makes my skin crawl.

I know Frances survived in spite of me, not because of me.

And I have spent every waking moment of her life since making it up to her. Making it up to Liz and Tommy. Maybe even Sandy Weaver and her unborn baby.

With the pie in the oven, I eat a lunch of tomato soup and a grilled cheese sandwich, and I feed Liz pureed ham and peas that look and smell like jarred baby food. I fold a small basket of laundry, pay a few bills with the checkbook, and put

Liz on the commode, which can be a forty-five minute job some days.

By late afternoon, I am to the point in my day I dread most, that idle time before dinner when there are no more tasks to keep my hands busy. I wheel Liz into the living room in front of the picture window, where we have a full view of the farm down the road, and I sit in a chair next to her with a hat I am knitting for one of my four grandboys—Nolan, who manages to have a runny nose from October to April. I've often thought that if my grandchildren were weeds, Nolan would be wild clover, pleasantly sweet in the middle, Adam would be a dandelion, bright and colorful but all over the place, and Billy would be a thistle, hardy but painful if you step on one.

A heavy, wet snow begins to fall and smear the glass, bending the silos and distorting the rooflines of the twin farmhouses.

"You know," I say, startling Liz after a prolonged silence. "Beatrice once told me that she and Eunice used to skinny-dip in the pond behind the hay barn late at night when everyone else was asleep." I pull out a crooked line of blue yarn and start it again. "I never once swam in that pond in all the years I lived there. Isn't that funny? Ice-skated, but never swam." One of the needles slips from my fingers and clatters onto the hardwood floor. My face reddens from the effort of leaning over to reach it.

"Beatrice and Eunice." I shake my head. "You never knew them, but they were quite a pair. I only knew Eunice a short time, though, since she died literally the day I met her." I tear open a new package of blue yarn and find the end. "Have you ever heard of such a thing? Meeting someone on the very day they die?"

Eunice Krenshaw. The mysterious, unhappy woman whose house, and other attributes, it seems, I have inhabited the majority of my life. I stare at the elegant peak of the front porch of my former home, barely visible in the fading light, and my eyes move to the small window situated just below the eaves. It is the window to the attic, where the steamer trunk of Eunice's secrets, curses, and ghosts has resided for decades, where I left behind my own contribution—Tommy's pale blue button-up shirt, and Sandy Weaver's pearl necklace nestled in the folds.

Of course, I still think of Tommy. Oh, Tommy. The place where so many twisted roads of my life both began and ended. I try not to dwell on the ugly things Liz said the night Frances was born. I try not to think that had there never been the farm, the mistress, there never would've been a good divide, fracturing my heart in two.

Sometimes, Tommy's memory feels like one of those phantom noises I used to hear in my sleep when I would awake with a start and swear I'd heard some vague, unidentifiable noise that turned out to be just a figment of my imagination. He feels like that now, a figment of my imagination, something that was never real.

But I try not to think about all that anymore. You lose the light when you chase the shadows, my mother used to say.

I see a small line of spittle dangling from Liz's chin and I reach out with a tissue to wipe it away. She lays her good hand to my wrist with surprising strength, and pulls me down to her level. Our eyes lock. Several seconds pass.

I know this look, have seen it on enough occasions to understand. She is telling me she knows. Even though she can't speak of it, she remembers. She remembers what I did the night Frances was born, twenty years ago to the day.

She remembers how I left them both to die.

It would do no good to tell her what my intentions were when I walked out of her house. It would do no good to tell her that after some time had passed, while sitting in the icy rain wearing Sandy Weaver's pearls with a knife pressed to my own wrist, I finally came to my senses and ran back inside. That I had telephoned Jim with shaking fingers, crying for help, praying aloud over and over, *God forgive me, God forgive me, God forgive me.*

It wouldn't do anyone any good, so I wait, as I always do, until the look in her eyes softens. She blinks and turns back to the window. Finally, she releases me.

I vaguely recall, once upon a time, thinking of Liz as a redbud tree. What I had failed to realize, in my rush to judgment, is that redbud trees are some of the hardiest ornamentals around. She survived me, after all.

I return to little Nolan's blue scarf and resume knitting.

It is a great irony that when I first met Liz, I thought we were so different, when really, we were so much alike. We lived in the same house, on the same farm, shared the same daughter, loved the same man.

The afternoon light begins to fade. It will be dinnertime soon. I wonder if Frances will call like she promised in her letter. It would be a treat to hear her voice.

From the pocket of my sweater, I remove Will's old tortoise shell handle knife. I open the blade and cut the yarn at a good stopping point. It is a comfort to always have it in my pocket, even if I now only use it to cut my yarn.

"Time to get dinner on the table." I bundle and tuck the scarf into a wicker basket along with the needles, and then stand and stretch my stiff legs. The snow falls harder. Liz shivers. I unfold her favorite afghan and tuck it around her shoulders.

"There's a bowl of potato salad in the fridge I made yesterday," I say.

Liz doesn't hear me. She has nodded off once again.

I smile and say to myself, "Tommy always did love my potato salad."

ACKNOWLEDGMENTS

A special thank you to:

The fabulous team at MG Press, especially Robert James Russell and Jeff Pfaller, and editor Michelle Webster-Hein.

The talented Waukee broads, Wendy Delsol, Kim Stuart, Dawn Mooradian, Chantal Corcoran, and Dame Murl Pace.

Jane Ann Soetmelk for opening up the Magic House in Woodbine so I could work in peace and quiet, and Tracey Kelley, Sally Boekholt and so many others from the old Ya-Ya days who read bad early drafts.

Developmental editors Catherine Knepper and Jamie Chavez for generously reading and giving suggestions when I was hopelessly stuck.

Joy Azmitia for fighting so long and hard for this book.

The Key West Literary Seminar and the Iowa Arts Council for giving me vital support and funding.

My husband, Troy. My children, Drake, Seth, and Gauri. My reasons, always.

And a most special thank you to the divine Ms. Jackie Jensen: editor, mentor, reader, friend. You were my first real fan and your belief in me has done more for my writing than you'll ever know.

Kali VanBaale was born and raised on a dairy farm in rural southern Iowa. Her debut novel, *The Space Between* earned an American Book Award, the Independent Publisher's silver medal for general fiction, and the Fred Bonnie Memorial First Novel Award. Her short stories and essays have appeared in *The Milo Review*, *Northwind Literary*, *The Writer* and the anthologies *Voices of Alzheimer's* and *A Cup of Comfort for Adoptive Families*.

Her third novel, *The Cure for Hopeless Causes*, was awarded a State of Iowa Arts Council major artist grant and is currently pending publication. In 2014 she was awarded the Great River Writer's Retreat to begin work on a fourth novel.

Kali holds an MFA in creative writing from Vermont College of Fine Arts and has been an assistant professor of writing and literature at Drake University and Upper Iowa University. She currently lives and writes outside Des Moines with her husband and three children.